Calypso in London

Sam Selvon

Calypso in London

PENGUIN CLASSICS
an imprint of
PENGUIN BOOKS

PENGUIN CLASSICS

UK | USA | Canada | Ireland | Australia
India | New Zealand | South Africa

Penguin Books is part of the Penguin Random House group of companies
whose addresses can be found at global.penguinrandomhouse.com.

Stories originally published in *Ways of Sunlight* by MacGibbon & Kee 1957
This selection published in Little Clothbound Classics 2023
001

Copyright © Samuel Selvon, 1957

Cover design and illustration by Coralie Bickford-Smith

Set in 10/14.5pt Baskerville 10 Pro
Typeset by Jouve (UK), Milton Keynes
Printed and bound in Great Britain by Clays Ltd, Elcograf S.p.A.

The authorized representative in the EEA is Penguin Random House Ireland,
Morrison Chambers, 32 Nassau Street, Dublin D02 YH68

A CIP catalogue record for this book is available from the British Library

ISBN: 978-0-241-63087-7

Contents

Contents

Trinidad

Wartime Activities

One time in Trinidad during the war one set of thing happen to me, that afterwards I had was to hold my head and bawl. I mean, it going to sound as if I making up the story, but if I lie I die!

We uses to live on a sugar-cane estate name La Romain, and this crop season we was cutting the cane and carting it to the sugar factory. Was a set of Indians living on the estate, and all of we was labourers, sweating in the sun for a few dollars to buy flour and rice in the shop. From the time I was a little fellar I was working on the estate. Never been to school or anything. But don't think I was foolish. I uses to borrow books and magazines from the overseer and study learning. My old man say that is only a waste of time, that I should be bathing the hog-cattle in the pond or fixing the harness on the cart instead of trying to read book, but whenever I had a chance I studying learning.

Well this crop season they put up a bonus for the fellars who could cut the most canes, and I was out in the fields with my cutlass and swiping cane until the sun went down, trying to earn that extra money.

Well I didn't know anything, but the old man and old lady was making plans for me behind my back. Indian parents like to married off their children early, and it look as if the old man was thinking it was time they fix up a married thing for me, in real Indian fashion, which was to make a match with the parents of some girl that I ain't ever see in my life.

The old man went up to Chaguanas that day and come home late in the evening. Chaguanas was a town about twenty-twenty-five miles from where we was living. And when he come back, he bust the mark.

'*Betah*,' he say, 'I notice these days like you not settle in your mind, I think you coming big man now, and is time you get wife.'

I waiting cool to hear what it is he have on his mind.

'So *betah*,' he go on, 'we make a match for you with a nice girl in Chaguanas. She father have a lot of money and land, so you will get a lot of present at the ceremony.'

'Don't worry with me and that sort of thing,' I say. 'If you think I going married a girl that I ain't even see, you make a mistake.'

'You better don't argue with me,' he say. 'You coming a big man now. You think I didn't see you laying down in the cane with Rookmin daughter last week?'

'I wasn't doing anything,' I say.

'But like you wanted to,' he say. 'Anyway, this thing done settle.'

'This is a modern world,' I say, 'and you can't do thing like that any more.'

'You reading too much book,' he say, and with that he went out to smoke pipe and talk with the neighbours.

I don't know what you would of done in my position, but I know what I did. I didn't talk to him any more about the matter, but when the crop season was over and I get my bonus, bam! I pack up a few things and I out off from the estate and went to San Fernando, which is the brightest town the island have in the south.

This was the first time in my life I ever left the

estate, but I didn't want to appear like no country-bookie, so I walking about like I is the heppest man in town. But this time so I frighten to see so much traffic and people moving about, and to hear people talking about the war as if it was going on next door.

I rent a cheap room in Mucurapo Street, which part all the sports uses to hang out, and I get a job in the oilfields in Point-à-Pierre, about two-three miles away.

It was fine in Mucurapo Street. I get in with the sports and I had to regulate my nights with them. Some of them calling me little boy and force-ripe mango, but all the same I was holding the fort in a big way. One night I just finish seeing a double at the Palace behind the library and I was standing up by the roundabout when a test broach me and say he was bawling, that he come from Port of Spain to see somebody, and now he stranded and can't find no place to sleep. He say that up in town – meaning Port of Spain – he is a hero, but down here he don't know nobody and he don't know if to bounce a sleep on a bench on Harris Promenade or if to go down by the wharf and look for a fishing boat drawn up on the beach.

I ease him up, and let him sleep by me for the night, and next morning he tell me his name was Little One, and that if I ever come up to town I must look him up, though he ain't have a fixed place of abode.

It was about two months after that episode that I get tired with the oilfield work where I was only catching my tail, and I tell the boss to go to hell one morning. They give me a week's wages and tell me to peel off. All the sports in Mucurapo Street sympathise with me, and they want to keep me until things get right, but I was remembering Little One and I had a hankering for the big city.

So I take the midday train and it was crowded for so with all kind of frowsy people. When we reach Port of Spain I get out and start to walk up Frederick Street looking at people. Up here was worse than San Fernando with business and bustling and hustling, and I feel like a fish out of water and I mad to catch the next train back for South.

But while I stand up there thinking who should I see but Little One, doing a window-shop with a sharp piece of skin. As soon as he see me he shout out: 'What you doing here, coolie? Your area is down South.'

So I tell him how things was brown with me and I hear that in town Yankee dollar falling all about.

Little One say: 'You could buy two beers?'

I feel in my pocket and though I don't want to spend no money foolish, I tell him yes. So he give the thing he was with a small walk and we went and sit down and had six beers.

Little One tell me that he could fix up a job for me as a pilot. He say how it have plenty of Yankee and Limey who does come from the ships, and is according to how many of them I could pilot that I would get pay. With that, Little One want to peel off and leave me, but I tell him to hold a key, that it was the first time I ever in Port of Spain, and how I would know where to go and what to do?

'You talking so hep,' Little One say, 'that I thought you born in the town. Go around by Mavis, and she will fix you up. Tell she Little One send you.'

He tell me where to find Mavis, and I went to look for she.

Mavis was living in Charlotte Street, in one of them grim backyard it have there. She was washing clothes in a tub of nasty water in the yard when I reach. I could see the big breasts as she bend to scrub the clothes and I remember the sports in Mucurapo Street and the sun being very hot and everything the first thing I find myself saying is how about a piece.

'Man you damn fast,' Mavis say fiercely, looking up. When she look up it ain't make much difference with the breasts: they pushing out of the bodice as if they on the mark for a race. 'What you mean by coming in my yard in the first place, I made to call a policeman for you.'

That cool me off and I explain how Little One send me, and Mavis say to go inside and sit down, she coming just now.

Mavis room was a kind of four wall, window, chair-and-table, double-bed affair, with the paint peeling off all about. It remind me of the room I had in San Fernando. It had a coal-pot in a corner and something was cooking.

When Mavis come in I tell she how I was working with Little One, and that he send me round by her to get all the lowdown. Same time I ask she if I could stay until I manage to get a room somewhere. She say she had a man already, that he name Dumboy, that if Little One thought she was some blasted boarder and lodger.

'So how you could hustle if you have a man?' I ask.

'Dumboy have a work with the Yankees in Chaguaramas Bay,' Mavis say, 'and he working nights. Right now he must be loafing round by the market, so you best hads go and come back about six o'clock, else if Dumboy catch you here he beat you like a snake.'

She begin to stir the pot and I smell calaloo.

'How about some food,' I say.

'You best hads go,' Mavis say. 'If Dumboy come he go make big trouble.'

Well the old man don't know what to do, but anyway, I start to breeze around town, then I went in Woodford Square and sit down. Two fellars was arguing about the war, how it look like Germany winning, and how it have so much Yankee in Trinidad now.

I listen to them a little bit, then I went in a café in Duke Street and eat a rock-cake and drink a mauby. Afterwards I went to a 1.30 show at the Empire and they was showing Alan Ladd in *This Gun for Hire*, but after a few reels I was sweating like a horse so I left the theatre and take a tramcar and went for a ride round the savannah.

It was a lovely evening though a bit cloudy and I

get out by the Rock Gardens and watch them children
and nursemaids and couples making love.

Them nursemaids, they wasn't paying any attention to the children: they only sit down on the grass
bad-talking their employers and only now and then
one shout out to a child who was playing too near
the pond. What happen was a little girl bend down
to see if she could see any fish in the pond and she
fall in the water. Lucky thing, I was sitting down on
a rock near by and I haul the child from the water.

You should hear all them nursemaids.

'The child too stubborn!'

'These white children don't like listen!'

'Good thing the mister was there to haul she out!'

Everybody crowd around and the nursemaid in
charge of the child only looking around and saying:
'But what I will tell the madam when we go back?'
She take off the wet shoes and socks and dress and
spread them out to dry, and she make the child sit
down on the grass and lifting her hand threateningly
to make the child stop crying.

Well I sizing up the nursemaid, because she don't
look so bad at all, and to beat everything she is Indian
like me. She have long hair and a coca-cola-bottle

figure, and she cursing the child in Hindi, though I
is the only one there who know that. I so glad to hear!
Right away I start to prattle in Hindi too.

'What your name?' I ask.

'Doolarie,' the thing answer.

'You working for white people?' I ask.

'Yes,' she say. 'They living round by St Clair. I just
come to take the child for a walk.'

'Which part you come from?'

'I come from Chaguanas,' she say.

After the children begin to play again we went and
sit down under a poui tree and the flowers was falling
and she was picking them up and making chain as
we talk. She tell me that she run away from home,
but when I ask she why she wouldn't say. Then she
ask me where I working and I say I have a big job
with the Yankees.

The thing looking innocent and pretty and the old
man feeling that this is really a sharp craft, and making old-talk and trying to hold her hand, though
everytime I do that she pull the hand away.

Doolarie get up to see if the clothes dry, and I sit
down watching her, biting grass and thinking that

this was the first time I ever meet a thing that I really fall for, and look at my position!

Doolarie dress the child and stand up by the tram-stop waiting. I ask her what she doing tonight and she say nothing, but the old man can't follow up because he have work to do.

I went on the tram and I pay the fares and tell her I was sorry, but that I working in the night because ships were in, and in a way that was the truth.

'You coming back by the Rock Gardens tomorrow evening?' I ask.

'Yes,' Doolarie say.

'I go try to come,' I say.

She give me a nice smile as I hop off the tram and I feel hearts.

Well that night was very fruitful for Little One and his setup. I went by Mavis and she give me something to eat, and when it was hunting time the both of we cut out for Park Street. All this time I worrying about Dumboy, if he suspect Mavis and make a tack back from work and find we hustling. And also I remembering Doolarie, and wishing I had a good job and a nice place to live, because I really fall for the thing.

I mean, if my father did want me to get married to a thing like Doolarie, I wouldn't mind.

Two Yankee destroyers and a British cruiser was in port that night, so you could imagine what the city like. By Green Corner you couldn't count the Limeys, and this time so you only seeing uniform all about the place.

We stop three Yankee and start to talk business but a policeman come up and say to get a move on else he put we up for loitering. Right away Mavis want to fight and curse the policeman, but I hold on to her hand and pull she away, and the Yankees follow up behind. In a little side street we stand up talking and then Mavis hail a taxi and all of we get in it, heading for Barataria, which was a little village where Little One had headquarters, town being too hot for him.

When we get up there we went in a small house off the main road. Like a jam session was going on there. Little One and four-five of his men passing drinks to all kind of uniform. You would think it was a serviceman club. A radio was playing 'They Wouldn't Believe Me' and Little One with a bottle of Vat 19 in his hand, going around and pouring some heavy drink. But I ain't see no girls, and when I ask Mavis she say they in the back room.

After a few minutes the Yankees and the Limeys begin to argue about who should go in the back room first. The Limeys say bloody Yankees and the Yankees say Limey bastards and it look like a big fight was going to start up.

Anyway, Little One hustle in the Yankees first, because a dollar is a dollar, and the Yanks like they was holding big. Then afterwards the Limeys went, but when they come back I could see like they wasn't satisfied, and they went outside in the road and begin to argue with the Yanks.

All this time, the old man feeling uncomfortable, only remembering the nice piece of skin he see in the gardens, and I can't settle down at all. Little One come up and ask me what happen, but I only shrug my shoulders and turn away.

By the time Mavis was ready to go back to Port of Spain, a big fight start up outside, between America and Britain. It was a one-sided thing, because it had more Yanks than Limeys.

'They taking advantage,' I say.

'You better leave the fight and come go home,' Mavis say.

A Yankee lift up a Limey like he was a child and

throw him in the air. When I see that, my blood get hot, and I went in and start to fling wild cuff and kick all about the place. The Yanks must be think that all the local boys coming to fight because all of them stop and begin to pick up hat and cap, and the fight finish right there.

Well I went back home with Mavis, and all this time I only studying Doolarie. Suddenly I want to get out of the city and back to the canefields and the open air and the sun. So that when we was on the bed I just lay there watching up at the cobwebs and scratching. Though Mavis had a busy night like she still wanted to go a rounds, but with Doolarie on my mind I only roll over on the other side and went to sleep.

Next morning I crawl out of bed and put on my clothes. Mavis get up while I was dressing and she thirsty for a rounds, but the old man say no. She get damn vex at that and tell me to get to hell out, that she would put Dumboy on my trail and get him to beat me up.

I went in a Chinese teashop and had a cup of coffee and a ham sandwich.

Sitting down there by a dirty table, I feel as if my

whole life toppling down on me, as if I ain't worth anything.

Same time a test come in and ask for a quick coffee, and though nobody ask him why he want it quick, is as if he feel he had to say why, and after saying 'A quick coffee, Ling,' he went on: 'I have to catch a bus, I hear the Americans taking on fellars in Chaguaramas.'

When I hear that, I decide that things so bad with me already that they couldn't be worse, and I catch a bus and went down to the Yankee base.

It had a long line of fellars line up in the gallery of a big building mark Employment Here and I join the line like I knew what it was all about. Pretty soon a Yankee officer come out and look at we as if we is cattle. One by one fellars begins to go in the office, and when it come my turn I walk in brazen.

It had a good-looking sport sitting behind a desk and she hand me a piece of paper and ask me what was my line of work. The first thing that come in my head is mechanic, so I say that. From there I went to another thing who take my fingerprints. Then they send me in another room, where it had fellars with their clothes off, waiting to see the doctor. All of we line up and going up to the doctor one by one, and the doctor sounding the chest and saying, 'O.k., o.k.'

Afterwards they send me to the Mechanic Foreman and he say twenty bucks a week. 'Look at that engine there,' he say, 'and when the oil gauge drops put in oil and so on.'

Well it had a chair and I sit down, looking at this gauge. That was about half-past ten in the morning. Twelve o'clock come, and the gauge ain't drop. I went in the canteen and buy a hotdog and a packet of Camels and come back.

By the time the siren blow at four o'clock, the gauge ain't fall, and my bottom hot from sitting down and doing sweet f—all.

A fellar come to take over and I ask him about it.

'What you worrying about, old man,' he say, 'you getting the Yankee money to scratch your tail. If the gauge don't fall, it just don't fall. I working here two weeks now and the gauge never fall.'

Back in Port of Spain, I barely had time to catch a tram and go by the Rock Gardens to look and see if Doolarie come to keep the date we make. I went and sit down the same place, on a rock near the pond. Though it have plenty people coming and going, I can't see my thing in the crowd at all. I must be smoke about ten Camels waiting there.

By now it starting to get dark, and I sure she ain't coming, but still I fooling myself that she would come. You see how it is in life? I mean, Doolarie really inspire me to go and look for a decent work and try to make something of myself, and now I was trying and bam! she out off and I can't see her nowhere, I don't even know which part she working, else I could of breezed around by the house and whistle or something.

I didn't have nothing to do but go back to town and lean up on a lamp-post and meditate on life as I eat a piece of watermelon. By and by I went around by Piccadilly to look for a cheap room, and I manage to get one for four dollars a month – that is to tell you what kind of room it was! It had a canvas cot to sleep on, and nothing else at all.

I lay down on the cot thinking hard, but the thoughts wouldn't make no sense. I try to sleep, but a steel band was practising 'Canaan Barrow' by the Dry River and they was making noise like hell.

I get up and went out, walking about with no aim. Near to Royal Theatre it had a donkey-cart with coconut and a Indian fellar opening the nuts with a sharp cutlass. I just start to sport a coconut water – I barely put the nut to my mouth – when I hear a familiar voice and it was shouting: 'That is the man, Dumboy, that is the coolie who force me to sleep with him!'

And before I know what happening in truth, this test Dumboy push the coconut out of my hand and start to beat blows on me, and a crowd gather and start to shout: 'Heave, heave, heave calalay heave!'

Dumboy have on brass knuckles and he only hitting and hitting. I try to grab the coconut from the ground to bust it on his head but when I bend down he raise his knee and it collide with my head and I went tumbling.

I don't know what would of happen there that night if a policeman didn't appear and hold on to me, I think I would of killed Dumboy with blows, even though he was beating me like a snake.

Well I spend the night in a cell, and next morning they take us before the magistrate. Before I have time to say anything the magistrate say: 'I deem you a rogue and a vagabond, thirty dollars or one month's imprisonment.'

Lord, which part I could get thirty dollars from? 'Take him away,' the magistrate say.

I don't know what happen to Dumboy. Mavis was in court and the last thing I hear was she shouting out something to the magistrate. As for me, I find myself in the cell again.

The next day I write my father and tell him to come quick and bring the money with him. When he come, he starting to make all kind of condition, how if he get me out I mustn't run away again, and how I would have to get married. I say yes yes to all that because the only thing I was studying was to get out and get back to where I could feel the wind on my face.

Well a few days after all this my father went up Chaguanas to fix up this married thing. When he come back, he look as if he worried.

'What happen?' my mother ask him.

'The girl run away,' he say, 'but they know which part she is, and they going to bring she back home.'

This time so, working in the cane-fields, I forget all about Doolarie, and I did already make up my mind to follow whatever pattern my old man set for me.

About a week later everything ready for the marriage. It have all kind of ceremony in Indian wedding.

The parents does offer you all kind of thing, cattle and house and money and so on. But the hurtful part is that the girl you going to married have she face cover up, same as you, and the two of you don't know who the other is. But it had a part of the ceremony where the two of you have to get under a sheet while the priests doing their business, and you should know that when it was time for that, I had a peep at the girl under the sheet.

Doolarie always uses to say, after we did settle down in we own house, that people wouldn't believe when we tell them. But all them things really happen to me while the war was fighting, and if I lie I die.

Holiday in Five Rivers

When it was the last day of school Popo put his copy-book and food-carrier in the satchel his mother had made for him from a piece of coloured cotton, and he waited at the gate for Govind, his big brother, and together they took the stony trail that led four miles over hill and valley to Five Rivers.

The road didn't seem as stony as usual, because the school was going to be closed a long time for repairs.

Popo was full of excitement.

'Plenty holiday, we will have time to do plenty things.' Govind, twelve years old, was just as enthusiastic, but all the same he said to Popo:

'Plenty things, yes! But I warning you from in front, that I don't want you hanging around my tail all the time. You still a little boy, and you must play with children your age.'

'I won't do anything, Govind.' The little boy held on to his brother's hand and looked up entreatingly. 'I just want to be with you, because you always doing brave things, and I getting big now, too besides.'

Govind flung Popo's grip off his hand. 'Ah, you too small to have any sense, you always making noise, or starting to cry and say you want to go home. You remember the time when we did went to thief in Procop garden? What happen? When the watchman see us, everybody run, but you sit down and start to cry.'

'But that was long time,' Popo walked backwards in front of his brother to talk face to face. 'I promise you this time I will do whatever you say. And you remember the time when Pa was putting a cock and some rice at the cross roads to work obeah, ain't it was I who did tell you about it?'

'Ah, and you remember the time when Pa did ask who it was that burst the strap for the donkey saddle, ain't it was you who tell him that it was me?'

'But you remember the time when you did run away from school to go and fish cascadura in the river, I didn't say nothing then, though.'

They walked along the rugged trail, trading

memories in a fierce argument, until at last, as they got to the small hill overlooking Five Rivers, Govind said:

'All right, but I warning you in front, the first time you make a mistake, I not going to take you anywhere where I go.'

From where they were now, the village looked like it was in a basin at their feet. High green hills, covered with lush vegetation, surrounded the village, and when it was the season of pouis these flowers showed like yellow blobs decorating the hillsides. But there was always colour besides the stagnant green, for if immortelles' crimson blossoms were absent here and there were blooms of perennial wild tropical plants.

Far in the Northern Range a river started, and when it got to the valley of Five Rivers it broke up because of the lie of the land, and there were five little streams which flowed near the village, giving it its name.

The peasants lived simply, out of touch with happenings in other parts of Trinidad, in a little world where food and shelter and a drink in Chin's shop on Saturday night were all the requisites for existence.

In that one shop anything from a bottle of rum to

a safety pin could be bought. It was owned and run by Chin, a fat Chinaman. Chin was so much in demand that he never left the shop except to visit the nearest town on Sundays to see some friends and have a smoke of opium. When he did that, the shop remained closed until his return late on Monday morning. So that on a Saturday night every man, woman and child was there, and it was like a regular bazaar with shouting and drinking and smoking and gossiping.

When they had indulged in all the usual activities, like hunting birds and squirrels or bathing in one of the streams, Govind and Popo began to find the holidays dull. These were things they did all the time, school or no school.

Then one morning Chin spread a canvas awning in front of the shop to keep out the rays of the sun. Under this awning there was a wooden veranda where sometimes women sold sweets and cakes.

When Chin did that, More Lazy decided to migrate from under the spreading samaan tree in the centre of the village and go to live on Chin's veranda. This transplanting of his body caused More Lazy some concern, as it entailed the use of his own energy to walk the hundred-odd yards to the shop. But for some time he had noticed that the samaan tree protected him from the heat only in the morning. From noon, as the sun travelled west, it threw rays under the tree and on to More Lazy where he lay dozing.

Govind and Popo and the other children stopped pitching marbles in amazement as More Lazy got up and stretched under the samaan tree.

'Look! Look More Lazy getting up!' they shouted, and they began to tease the old negro.

In the whole of Five Rivers, or the whole of Trinidad for that matter, there was not another man lazier than More Lazy, and when he moved from under the samaan tree it was the subject of much conversation. They have it to say in the village that once Mr Dosanto, the plantation overseer, went into the shop to buy a drink, and on leaving accidentally dropped a dollar bill near to where More Lazy was, not knowing anything. They say it fell within a foot of More Lazy, and all he had to do was stretch out his hand and put it away without saying a word. But instead he kept an eye on it and waited until someone was passing by, then he asked for the person to bend down and pick it up for him, please.

It was only once a year that he stirred and came to life. That was during Carnival, the two-day festival before Ash Wednesday. More Lazy would bestir himself and journey into the capital of Port of Spain to take part in the celebrations. And while others were content to disguise themselves as pirates or Arabian sheikhs, he, strangely enough, had to enjoy himself in a more active impersonation, and would get someone to team up with him to play 'police and thief', he playing the part of a policeman chasing a thief through the streets of the city.

Accompanied by jeers and taunts from the children, More Lazy accomplished the journey to Chin's shop and established himself in a corner with a loud sigh, his body falling wearily to the ground.

The children stood at a distance and teased him, and Govind threw a stone. But More Lazy was unresponsive and they went off to pitch marbles again.

The dry season came and the boys set traps for ground-doves. In the brown bush, they bent limbs and made bows, and attached strings with loops.

But Govind tired of pastimes which didn't call for risks, and for two days, whenever Popo came near to him, he pushed his small brother away, sneering at any suggestion he offered to pass the time away as being childish and not worth the effort.

Then Popo surprised him by saying, 'I make friends with More Lazy, though.'

'How you do that?' Govind wanted to know, for they were always teasing the old man and he in turn threatened them if they came within reach.

'Oh, I do one or two little things for him, and now he and I is good friends, he tell me a secret.'

'What secret?' Govind asked disinterestedly, wishing with all his heart that a bush fire would break out or something.

'Well, it not really a secret. But he tell me a trick we could play on Jagroop.'

Jagroop was an old Hindu who lived on one of the hills, about half a mile up, where the forest was so thick that one was taken aback to come across the sudden clearing where his hut was. Jagroop had cut away the bush and built the hut himself, using bamboo from the river banks and palm leaves to thatch the roof. He made the walls with mud reinforced with dry grass and shrubs. Sometimes hunters passed near to Jagroop's place in the night, and he used to be so angry that he threatened to poison the river water and kill the whole village unless they stopped trespassing on his property.

Every Saturday he passed through the village with the panniers of his donkey laden with fruits and vegetables. He never stopped on his way out to the bigger village of Sans Souci. He said the people in Five Rivers were too cheap, that he couldn't make any profit selling to them.

But when he got back in the evening he would regularly tie his donkey outside Chin's shop and stand up for a few minutes to curse More Lazy, saying that it was a shame that he slept all day while other people had to work hard. Then he would enter the shop and proceed to get drunk.

It was a weekly pattern with him. He was tight with his money, no one knew what he did with all the money he made trading. He didn't spend it all on rum, for after one bottle he was so drunk that some kindly villager had to put him on the donkey and send him home.

'Well, tell me, what trick it is?' Govind asked.

'First you must promise to take me with you,' Popo said.

'All right. What is the trick?'

Popo went close to his brother although they were alone and whispered in his ear. Govind's face brightened.

'Tonight self we will do it. You and me, and Lal and Harry could come too if they like.'

That night the boys stole an empty coffin and placed it in front of Jagroop's hut. They screamed and made all sorts of horrifying noises and hid in the bushes to see what would happen.

Jagroop flung open the door, cursing loudly in Hindi. When he saw the coffin, instead of backing away in fear he gave it a kick. Then he went inside and came back with a cutlass and he hacked the coffin to pieces, swearing all the time.

'Ah, that was a stupid idea,' Govind said afterwards, 'he didn't do anything, he wasn't frighten at all.'

They were all disappointed at the result, and a few days later when Popo told Govind, 'More Lazy tell me another trick to play on Jagroop,' Govind said:

'Ah, you never have any good ideas. I going to fish with Lal, and I don't want you to come.'

'But listen, this is a good trick . . . well, it not a trick really. Is to look for treasure.'

'Treasure? Who would have treasure in Five Rivers, where everybody so poor?'

'Well, don't be so impatient, man. But promise to take me first.'

'All right, but I hope is something good More Lazy tell you this time.'

'You know how Jagroop always selling plenty provisions, and how he is a stingy man. More Lazy say how he sure that Jagroop have plenty money hide up some place, and that we could look for it. He say that he would go himself, but is only that he does be so tired.'

'You mean lazy,' Govind said. But he thought about the idea, and the more he thought about it, the more appealing it seemed to him.

'All right! We will look all about for it!'

Govind felt it was a challenge to his ability, and in a short time he had mustered a gang of boys and they set about to look for the Indian's money.

Likely spots in and around the village were dug up. One Saturday evening while Jagroop was getting drunk Govind even ventured into the hut and ripped away the floorboards. They set a night and day watch on Jagroop, spying on him as he worked on his plot or pottered about the yard.

But search high, search low, there was no discovering where the Indian had hidden his money, though More Lazy, having nothing to do, would get up after a doze and say he had dreamed where the money was hidden, and send them off on a wild goose chase.

For a week they kept at it, and then Govind said:

'Ah, that was another stupid idea. We can't find out where Jagroop have that money hide.'

The dry season was now at its height. The five streams around the village were mere trickles, not more than a foot wide or a couple of inches deep in places, and the villagers had to dig canals for the water to flow into one main channel.

Even More Lazy seemed affected, and he now lay with an earthen goblet of water and a tin can near him, so he could ask Popo to pour him a drink to quench his thirst.

It happened that most of the fruit trees around were bare except for a mango tree in Jagroop's garden which looked like it had sucked all the life from the other trees, for it was in full fruit, and from a distance the boys could see the red mangoes dangling on their stems.

Govind planned an 'attack' on this tree, so one

morning with the leaves so dry and crisp they crackled like shells underfoot, he and Popo crept into the garden.

There was no sign of Jagroop, and this roused rather than allayed their fear. However, they managed to get behind the hut—making a wide circle to avoid it—and right under the mango tree.

Govind hoisted Popo up and soon they were at the top of the tree feasting on the fruit, Popo having brought a penknife and pepper and salt with which to eat the green ones.

They had filled their pockets and bosoms and were just about to descend when Popo held Govind's arm in a tight grasp and pointed.

Below them the bush was so thick they couldn't see if someone was passing below, all they saw was the bushes shake.

It was Jagroop. Even though he was completely hidden he was walking in a sort of half crouch, a cutlass and tin clutched to his chest while one hand cleared the way of brambles. He stopped where one of the streams crawled through the land, and glancing all around, sat down on the bank and wet his cutlass and began to sharpen it on a stone.

He was now clearly seen by the boys, and it appeared to them that he was only pretending, or 'playing possum' as they used to say. For all the time he was watching the bushes, like a deer which had smelt man but wasn't sure where he was. And the boys got real scared, for it looked like he knew all the time they were up in the mango tree, and it looked too, the easy way he was sitting, that he was only waiting for them to climb down to give chase with his cutlass.

They scarcely dared breathe, and Govind could feel Popo's fingers squeezing and relaxing, squeezing and relaxing on his arm.

'You think he see we?' Popo's whisper was hot in Govind's ear.

'Let we wait and see what he go do,' Govind whispered back, no less afraid than his little brother.

Half an hour passed. Jagroop was humming a Hindi song as he moved the cutlass to and fro on the stone. The cutlass must have been as sharp as a razor, yet he went on. He struck it lightly at a hanging bamboo leaf. Then he tested the blade again by shaving an inch or two of hair off his leg.

And that seemed to satisfy him, for he got up at

last. Near to a large slab of rock which jutted out from the bank he stood up for a minute. Then muttering to himself he gathered stones, and he damned the thin trickle of water, digging earth from the bank with his cutlass.

And when the water ceased to flow, he began to dig in the bed of the stream itself.

The boys could see beads of perspiration glistening on his dark skin as he dug and dug, stopping at sudden moments and cocking his head sideways as dry leaves rustled or a dove flew noisily in the bush.

For another half an hour they hung suspended, as it were, on the branches of the mango tree.

Then Jagroop stopped digging and reached into the hole with his hands.

He brought out two tins and he sat down and opened them.

Sunlight fell on silver. Hundreds of shillings and two-shillings and half-crown pieces. They glinted and the boys could hear the ring as he let them trickle through his fingers and fall back into the tins.

Jagroop chuckled as he played with the money, entirely engrossed in his hoarding.

Govind saw now why they had been unable to discover the hiding place. Who would have dreamed of digging in the bed of a flowing stream? Not even More Lazy himself. Now, all the Indian had to do was bury the money and fill the hole firmly with stones and earth, and break the dam and the water would flow over the spot and keep the secret.

It was too good. It was too clever. They couldn't contain themselves. They were just bursting to reveal the secret.

Scrambling down the mango tree with an exciting elation, Govind and Popo set up a great shouting to give themselves courage, and jettisoning mangoes left and right from their pockets and bosoms, ran pell-mell down the hill to the village.

The Village Washer

Shortly after the last war the laundry situation took a turn for the worse in the village of Sans Souci, a sugar-cane hamlet thirty-odd miles from the capital of Port of Spain in Trinidad. Here Ma Lambee ruled supreme as the only washer in the district, and in her sole supremacy she grew careless after she had established herself.

Ma Lambee was old and black and possessed remarkable strength which seemed to bow her legs so she walked like a duck.

With the declaration of war, she began to be neglectful of collars and sleeves and the folds at the bottom of trousers, which places the villagers always looked to judge her workmanship. If a button broke or came off as she scrubbed the clothing with a corn husk, she no longer bothered to mend it, and if a thin shirt ripped as she kneaded her gnarled hands into the cloth, she swore the tear was there before she got the shirt. Was a time when she used four bars of blue soap, and if the dirt and perspiration were still stubborn, bought a bit of washing soda and did her best to get the clothes looking clean again. And was a time when she used four to six buckets of water for one tub of washing: now she used four buckets for two tubs.

Ma Lambee had four flat irons which she heated in a coal pot, wrapping a piece of cloth around the handle to protect her hand as she pressed the clothes. And a good job she did, too, until the war started. Then she bought half the amount of coals and stopped greasing the irons with lard when they were not in use. When she was ironing, she just slid the hot iron around quickly, folded the clothes and put them in the flat, wooden tray, and took them around on her head every Saturday to deliver the laundry.

However, Ma Lambee's excuse that there was a war on didn't stop the villagers from complaining. There were about forty of them living near the cane-fields where they worked, cutting the canes to be transported to the sugar mills two miles away. Of these, about ten did their own washing and the rest depended on Ma Lambee.

But the old woman paid no attention to the complaints. She always promised to do better the following week, but when she came around balancing the tray on her head, customers discovered all the dirt under the collars, and once a merino was so torn that the owner's wife asked her if it was a net to catch fish in the river, and refused to pay for it.

Ma Lambee was unperturbed. In fact, she was 'brazen enough', as a villager put it, to announce that she was raising laundry prices.

'As you know,' she told the women as she stopped at each hut to collect the dirty linen, 'we fighting a war, and the prices of all things going up. So from now on, I will have to charge more to do up the clothes. Long time a shirt was twelve cents. Now it have to be eighteen cents. And long time, skirt was eighteen cents. Now it have to be a shilling.'

From hut to hut, as Ma Lambee passed, words flew furiously.

'Neighbour, you hear about Ma Lambee, how she charging more to do up the clothes now? You can imagine that? And look how careless she getting, not even bothering to sew up a tear, or put back on a button!'

'Yes, is true! I only wish we had another washer in the village; she is the only one, that is why she getting on so!'

'Well, I for one going and try to do the washing myself, if I have time in the evening. The woman must be mad or something!'

'She say the war cause it – what war she talking about?'

A delegation of housewives visited Ma Lambee where she lived in a broken-down hut under a mango tree, and there was a great argument which lasted for two hours. At the end of that time, the women retreated making threats and shaking their fists at Ma Lambee, who had told them flatly that they could do their own nasty washing if they didn't like her terms.

She lost five customers the following week, but the others were forced to put up with her conditions. Ma Lambee smiled to herself as she went about her washing.

But while she was having her own way word of the villagers' plight reached another hamlet called Donkey City, and another aged negro woman named Ma Procop migrated to Sans Souci with the hope of taking over the business from Ma Lambee.

The day Ma Procop arrived, she was greeted with shouts and smiles, though the people were cautious not to commit themselves too much, fearing she might turn out to be a second Ma Lambee.

But Ma Procop was a clever woman. The first day she put up a notice in the village shop, saying that she was willing to take in laundry at pre-war prices. She said she was an experienced washer from Donkey City and was out to give complete satisfaction to one and all.

It was a long notice, and the spelling was bad and it wasn't worded exactly that way, but the three people in the village who could read saw it and soon everybody knew.

When Ma Lambee heard about it she waddled over to the shop and stuck up a big piece of cardboard on which she had had the village painter write a few words in red paint, stating that she was negotiating with a firm in the city for a new type of washing machine which would make old clothes look like new.

There was no electricity in the village, and it was a lie anyway, but for the first time in her life Ma Lambee was afraid of losing her trade.

That Saturday as she made her rounds she did not

get even a vest to wash. Within a week she had lost all her customers. She was jeered at and the new washing machine became a big joke. Even the children made fun of her, shouting out 'Wash-up washer!' when they saw her.

If Ma Lambee saw Ma Procop walking down the road, she waddled over to the other side and turned her head as if she were smelling something bad. She looked upon the intruder as a hated enemy and thought up means of recovering her trade and at the same time putting Ma Procop to such shame that she would have to go back to Donkey City in a hurry.

At first she tried spreading lies.

'You know,' she told the women she met by the shop, 'that new washer is a nasty woman. She don't even rinse the clothes, and she look so sickly; take care she don't spread disease in the village!'

But Ma Procop's actions soon had the whole village on her side. She even spent a little out of the money she had saved in Donkey City, and worked late in the night sewing on buttons and mending torn clothing. And she made it her business to be friendly, and was especially kind to the children, buying sweets for them and telling them stories.

Ma Lambee now started a malicious rumour that Ma Procop was an obeah woman who changed herself into a bloodsucking animal in the night.

The simple-minded villagers, quick to superstition and belief in omens and evil spirits, became uneasy as the rumour took root.

One night a wounded animal ran into a backyard and left a trail of blood. Next morning Ma Lambee told them:

'Hm, it look like Ma Procop was working overtime last night. I don't know how you people could let that obeah woman live here.'

They began to imagine things. Night noises were attributed to an evil spirit, and though no one pointed directly to Ma Procop, there was an uneasy air whenever she was around. Quick to see her advantage, Ma Lambee pressed home the fact that the new washer was unusually fond of children – and that little ones were the favourites of obeah women.

She did more than talk. One night she poured a gallon of poison on to the roots of a big silkcotton tree in the centre of the village, and next day divined that as a result of Ma Procop's evil deeds the tree would die before a week passed.

She began to make a study of black magic in order to set the village against Ma Procop. She collected an odd miscellany of liquids and bones and other paraphernalia, and cleared her hut of mirrors and all objects in the sign of the cross.

Things came to a head when the silkcotton tree died. It just withered up, as Ma Lambee had predicted, and within two weeks it was nothing but a standing skeleton.

The village women got together to discuss the situation.

'It happen just as Ma Lambee say, it look like Ma Procop is really a obeah woman.'

'We have to put she to the test – get she to look in a mirror, and make the sign of the cross over she head. If she is really a obeah woman, she can't stand that at all.'

Ma Procop in the meantime was well aware of what was going on in the village. Yet she did nothing, except that one morning she went to Donkey City and came back with a parcel under her arm and a small smile on her lips.

Two days later, on a hot, sunshiny morning, a group of housewives came into Ma Procop's yard as she was hanging out the laundry on some makeshift lines between two mango trees. Ma Lambee was not among them, but while they were foregathering she had been telling them exactly what to do.

'Look in she house – I bet you wouldn't see any mirrors. And I bet you, too, that you find a lot of funny things in the house, like bone and bird feather and bottles and you might even find a skeleton.'

For Ma Lambee had done what she thought would be the last damning thing – she had sneaked into Ma Procop's hut and hidden all the stuff with which she had been practising her own evil acts, and she had removed the only mirror in the room, and a small crucifix near the head of the bed.

Ma Procop hung out a pair of khaki trousers and turned to face the women. They got to the point right away.

'Ma Procop,' the leader said, 'we hear that is you who working obeah in the village and causing evil spirit to walk about in the night.'

'What nonsense you talking?' she put her hands on her hips and looked outraged.

'Well, anyway, we going to search your house.'

They left her standing there and went into the hut.

A minute later bottles and bones came hurtling out the window.

'Is true! is true!' the women came tumbling from the hut in fear. 'You really working obeah! Look at all these things we find in your room!'

Ma Procop recovered quickly at this unexpected development.

'All these things you see here,' she waved her hands to the ground, 'they don't belong to me, I swear.' She made the sign of the cross with her two forefingers and kissed it loudly. 'They belong to Ma Lambee. I sure is she who put them in there, because she so spiteful since I come to the village and take away all the washing.'

The women began murmuring among themselves. Then suddenly one of them came forward and shoved a mirror in Ma Procop's face.

With a deliberate calm the washer said, 'Thank you,' and she fixed a piece of coloured cloth she wore on her head, looking straight into the mirror. Then, as if in a rage, she pulled the mirror and dashed it to the ground.

'That is the true test,' one in the group whispered, 'if she really obeah woman she can't look in a mirror.

Ma Lambee must be telling lie! It look as if Ma Procop not guilty!'

Ma Procop caught the turning of the tide. 'Listen,' she said. 'Let all of us go over by Ma Lambee and give she the test with a mirror and a cross. I have just what we need hide away inside the house, just give me a chance to get it.'

She dashed inside and came back with the parcel she had brought from Donkey City. She took the lead, heading straight for Ma Lambee's hut.

'You Ma Lambee,' she shouted as they got into the yard, 'you fooling people and saying that is I who working obeah, when is you all the time! Come out here in the yard let we test you!'

Ma Lambee came charging out of the hut. 'What you mean by keeping so much noise in my yard?' she demanded. She tried to keep a steady face but she knew that something had gone wrong.

'Look, we have a mirror and a cross here.' Ma Procop loosened the parcel and stepped ahead of the group. She moved quickly, and turned the mirror full in Ma Lambee's face, at the same time lifting the cross over her head.

No one heard the strange words Ma Procop was

fiercely whispering and the weird glint in her eyes, but everyone saw Ma Lambee cower in fear, and a look of extreme terror come into her face. She began to shake, as if she had ague. Then clasping her hands to her head she turned and ran shrieking into the hut.

Ma Procop turned to the frightened villagers.

'Nothing more to worry about,' she said in a tone of authority as she wrapped the mirror and cross into a parcel again. 'You will never have any obeah here as long as I stay in the village.'

The next morning Ma Procop stood by her hut watching Ma Lambee take the road to Donkey City, all her belongings wrapped in a sheet which she had slung over her shoulder.

As the old woman looked back for a last glimpse of Sans Souci she caught sight of Ma Procop leaning on the fencing, watching her.

With a yell of terror she waddled after her long shadow cast by the morning sun.

A Drink of Water

The time when the rains didn't come for three months and the sun was a yellow furnace in the sky was known as the Great Drought in Trinidad. It happened when everyone was expecting the sky to burst open with rain to fill the dry streams and water the parched earth.

But each day was the same; the sun rose early in a blue sky, and all day long the farmers lifted their eyes, wondering what had happened to Parjanya, the rain god. They rested on their hoes and forks and wrung perspiration from their clothes, seeing no hope in labour, terrified by the thought that if no rain fell soon they would lose their crops and livestock and face starvation and death.

In the tiny village of Las Lomas, out in his vegetable garden, Manko licked dry lips and passed a wet sleeve over his dripping face. Somewhere in the field a cow mooed mournfully, sniffing around for a bit of green in the cracked earth. The field was a desolation of drought. The trees were naked and barks peeled off trunks as if they were diseased. When the wind blew, it was heavy and unrelieving, as if the heat had taken all the spirit out of it. But Manko still opened his shirt and turned his chest to it when it passed.

He was a big man, grown brown and burnt from years of working on the land. His arms were bent and he had a crouching position even when he stood upright. When he laughed he showed more tobacco stain than teeth.

But Manko had not laughed for a long time. Bush fires had swept Las Lomas and left the garden plots charred and smoking. Cattle were dropping dead in the heat. There was scarcely any water in the village; the river was dry with scummy mud. But with patience one could collect a bucket of water. Boiled, with a little sugar to make it drinkable, it had to do.

Sometimes, when the children knew that someone had gone to the river for water, they hung about in the village main road waiting with bottles and calabash shells, and they fell upon the water-carrier as soon as he hove in sight.

'Boil the water first before drinking!' was the warning cry. But even so two children were dead and many more were on the sick list, their parents too poor to seek medical aid in the city twenty miles away.

Manko sat in the shade of a mango tree and tried to look on the bright side of things. Such a dry season meant that the land would be good for corn seeds when the rains came. He and his wife Rannie had been working hard and saving money with the hope of sending Sunny, their son, to college in the city.

Rannie told Manko: 'We poor, and we ain't have no education, but is all right, we go get old soon and dead, and what we have to think about is the boy. We must let him have plenty learning and come a big man in Trinidad.'

And Manko, proud of his son, used to boast in the evening, when the villagers got together to talk and smoke, that one day Sunny would be a lawyer or a doctor.

But optimism was difficult now. His livestock was dying out, and the market was glutted with yams. He had a great pile in the yard which he could not sell.

Manko took a look at his plot of land and shook

his head. There was no sense in working any more today. He took his cutlass and hoe and calabash shell which had a string so he could hold it dangling. He shook it, and realised with burning in his throat that it was empty, though he had left a few mouthfuls in it. He was a fool; he should have known that the heat would dry it up if he took it out in the garden with him. He licked his lips and, shouldering the tools, walked slowly down the winding path which led to his hut.

Rannie was cooking in the open fireplace in the yard. Sunny was sitting under the poui tree, but when he saw his father he ran towards him and held the calabash shell eagerly. Always when Manko returned from the fields he brought back a little water for his son. But this time he could only shake his head.

'Who went for water today by the river?' he asked Rannie.

'I think was Jagroop,' she answered, stirring the pot with a large wooden spoon, 'but he ain't coming back till late.'

She covered the pot and turned to him. 'Tomorrow we going to make offering for rain,' she said.

Next day, Las Lomas held a big feast, and prayers

were said to the rain god, Parjanya. And then two days later, a man called Rampersad struck water in a well he had been digging for weeks. It was the miracle they had been praying for. That day everyone drank their fill, and Rampersad allowed each villager a bucket of water, and Manko told Sunny: 'See how blessing doesn't only come from up in the sky, it does come from the earth, too.'

Rampersad's wife was a selfish and crafty woman, and while the villagers were filling their buckets she stood by the doorway of their hut and watched them. That night she told her husband he was a fool to let them have the water for nothing.

'They have money hide up,' she urged him. 'They could well pay for it. The best thing to do is to put barb' wire all round the well, and set a watchdog to keep guard in the night so nobody thief the water. Then say you too poor to give away for nothing. Charge a dollar for a bucket and two shillings for half-bucket. We make plenty money and come rich.'

When Rampersad announced this, the villagers were silent and aghast that a man could think of such a scheme when the whole village was burning away in the drought, and two children had died.

Rampersad bought a shotgun and said he would shoot anyone he found trespassing on his property. He put up the barbed wire and left a ferocious watch-dog near the well at nights.

As April went, there was still no sign in the sky. In Las Lomas, the villagers exhausted their savings in buying Rampersad's water to keep alive.

Manko got up one morning and looked in the tin under his bed in which he kept his money. There was enough for just two buckets of water. He said to Rannie: 'How long could you make two buckets of water last, if we use it only for drinking?'

'That is all the money remaining?' Rannie looked at him with fear.

He nodded and looked outside where the poui tree had begun to blossom. 'Is a long time now,' he said softly, 'a long time, too long. It can't last. The rain will fall, just don't be impatient.'

Rannie was not impatient, but thirst made her careless. It happened soon after the two buckets were empty. She forgot to boil a pan of river water, and only after she had drunk a cupful did she realise her fatal mistake. She was afraid to tell Manko; she kept silent about the incident.

Next day, she could not get out of bed. She rolled and tossed as fever ravaged her body.

Manko's eyes were wide with fright when he saw the signs of fever. Sunny, who had not been to school for weeks, wanted to do whatever he could, anything at all, to get his mother well so she could talk and laugh and cook again.

He spoke to his father after Rannie had fallen into a fitful sleep, with perspiration soaking through the thin white sheet.

'No money remaining for water, *bap*?'

Manko shook his head.

'And no money for doctor or medicine?'

He shook his head again.

'But how is it this man Rampersad have so much water and we ain't have any? Why don't we just go and take it?'

'The water belong to Rampersad,' Manko said. 'Is his own, and if he choose to sell it, is his business. We can't just go and take, that would be thiefing. You must never thief from another man, Sunny. That is a big, big, sin. No matter what happen.'

'But is not a fair thing,' the boy protested, digging

his hands into the brittle soil. 'If we had clean water, we could get *mai* better, not so?'

'Yes, *beta*,' Manko sighed and rose to his feet. 'You stay and mind *mai*, I going to try and get some river water.'

All day, Sunny sat in the hut brooding over the matter, trying hard to understand why his mother should die from lack of water when a well was filled in another man's yard.

It was late in the evening when Manko returned. As he had expected, the river was nearly dry, a foul trickle of mud not worth drinking. He found the boy quiet and moody. After a while, Sunny went out.

Manko was glad to be alone. He didn't want Sunny to see him leaving the hut later in the night, with the bucket and the rope. It would be difficult to explain that he was stealing Rampersad's water only because it was a matter of life or death.

He waited impatiently for Rannie to fall asleep. It seemed she would never close her eyes. She just turned and twisted restlessly, and once she looked at him and asked if rain had fallen, and he put his rough hand on her hot forehead and said softly no, but that he had seen a sign that evening, a great black cloud low down in the east.

Then suddenly her fever rose again, and she was delirious. This time he could not understand what she said. She was moaning in a queer, strangled way.

It was midnight before she fell into a kind of swoon, a red flush on her face. Manko knew what he must do now. He stood looking at her, torn between the fear of leaving her and the desperate plan that he had made. She might die while he was gone, and yet – he must try it.

He frowned as he went out and saw the moon like a night sun in the sky, lighting up the village. He turned to the east and his heart leapt as he saw the cloud moving towards the village in a slow breeze. It seemed so far away, and it was moving as if it would take days to get over the fields. Perhaps it would; perhaps it would change direction and go scudding down into the west, and not a drop of water.

He moved off towards the well, keeping behind the huts and deep into the trees. It took him ten minutes to get near the barbed wire fence, and he stood in the shadow of a giant silk-cotton tree. He leaned against the trunk and drew in his breath sharply as his eyes discerned a figure on the other side of the well, outside the barbed wire.

The figure stopped, as though listening, then began clambering over the fence.

Even as he peered to see if he could recognise who it was, a sudden darkness fell as the cloud swept over the moon in the freshening wind.

Manko cast his eyes upwards swiftly, and when he looked down again the figure was on the brink of the well, away from the sleeping watchdog.

It was a great risk to take; it was the risk Manko himself had to take. But this intrusion upset his plan. He could not call out; the slightest sound would wake the dog, and what it did not do to the thief, Rampersad would do with his shotgun.

For a moment, Manko's heart failed him. He smelt death very near – for the unknown figure at the well, and for himself, too. He had been a fool to come. Then a new frenzy seized him. He remembered the cruel red flush on Rannie's cheeks when he had left her. Let her die happy, if a drop of water could make her so. Let her live, if a drop of water could save her. His own thirst flared in his throat; how much more she must be suffering!

He saw the bucket slide noiselessly down and the rope paid out. Just what he had planned to do. Now draw it up, cautiously, yes, and put it to rest gently on the ground. Now kneel and take a drink, and put the fire out in your body. For God's sake, why didn't the man take a drink? What was he waiting for? Ah, that was it, but be careful, do not make the slightest noise, or everything will be ruined. Bend your head down . . .

Moonrays shot through a break in the cloud and lit up the scene.

It was Sunny.

'*Beta!*' Before he could think, the startled cry had left Manko's lips.

The dog sprang up at the sound and moved with uncanny swiftness. Before Sunny could turn, it had sprung across the well, straight at the boy's throat.

Manko scrambled over the fence, ripping away his clothes and drawing blood. He ran and cleared the well in a great jump, and tried to tear the beast away from the struggling boy. The dog turned, growling low in the throat as it faced this new attacker.

Manko stumbled and fell, breathing heavily. He

felt teeth sink into his shoulder and he bit his lip hard to keep from screaming in pain.

Suddenly the dog was wrenched away as Sunny joined the fight. The boy put his arms around the dog's neck and jerked it away from his father with such force that when the animal let go they both fell rolling to the ground.

Manko flung out his arm as he sprang up. In doing so, he capsized the bucket of water with a loud clang. Even in the struggle for life he could not bear to see the earth sucking up the water like a sponge. In fear and fury, he snatched the empty bucket and brought it down with all his strength on the dog's head.

The animal gave a whimper and rolled off the boy and lay still.

'Who that, thiefing my water?' Rampersad came running out into the yard, firing his shotgun wildly in the air.

'Quick, boy! Over the fence!' Manko grabbed the bucket and tossed it over. He almost threw Sunny to safety as the boy faltered on the wire. Then he half-dragged his own bleeding body up, and fell exhausted on the other side.

Sunny put his arm under his father and helped

him up. Together they ran into the shadow of the trees.

The noise of the gun and Rampersad's yells had wakened the whole village, and everyone was astir.

Father and son hid the bucket in a clump of dry bush and, waiting for a minute to recover themselves, joined the crowd which was gathering in front of Rampersad's hut.

Rampersad was beside himself with rage. He threatened them all with jail, screaming that he would find out who had stolen the water and killed the dog.

'Who is the thief? You catch him?' The crowd jeered and booed. 'It damn good. Serve you right.' Clutching his father's arm tightly, Sunny danced and chuckled with delight at Rampersad's discomfiture.

But suddenly silence and darkness fell together. A large black blob of cloud blotted out the moon. The sky was thick with clouds piling up on each other and there was a new coolness in the wind.

As one, the crowd knelt and prayed to the rain god. The sky grew black; it looked as if the moon had never been there. For hours they prayed, until Manko, thinking of Rannie, gently tapped his son and beckoned him away. They walked home hand in hand.

It was Sunny who felt the first drop. It lay on his hand like a diamond shining in the dark.

'*Bap?*' He raised questioning eyes to his father. 'Look!'

As Manko looked up, another drop fell on his face and rolled down his cheek. The wind became stronger; there was a swift fall of some heavy drops. Then the wind died like a sigh. A low rumble in the east; then silence. Perhaps Parjanya was having a joke with them, perhaps there would be no rain after all.

And then it came sweeping in from the north-east, with a rising wind. Not very heavy at first, but in thrusts, coming and going. They opened their mouths and laughed, and water fell in. They shouted and cried and laughed again.

Manko approached the hut where Rannie lay, and he was trembling at what he would find. He said to the boy: '*Beta*. You stay here. I go in first to see *mai*.' The boy's face went rigid with sudden fear. Though he was already drenched to the skin, he took shelter under the poui tree in the yard.

Manko was hardly inside the door when he gave a sharp cry of alarm. He thought he saw a ghostly figure tottering towards him, its face luminous-grey.

He flattened himself against the wall and closed his eyes. It was cruel of the gods to torment him like this. This was not Rannie: Rannie was lying in bed in the next room, she could not be alive any more.

'Manko.' It was her voice, and yet it was not her voice. 'What noise is that I hear? Is rain?'

He could not speak. Slowly, he forced himself to stretch out his hand and touch her forehead. It felt cold and unnatural.

He withdrew his hand, and began to tremble uncontrollably.

'Manko,' the lips formed the words. 'Manko, give me water!'

Something fell to the floor with a clatter. He saw that it was a tin cup, and that she had been holding it in her hand. She swayed towards him, and he caught her. Then Manko knew that it was a miracle. Rannie was shaking with cold and weakness, but the fever was gone, and she was alive.

Realisation burst upon him with such force that he almost fainted.

He muttered: 'I will get some for you.'

He picked up the cup and ran out into the lashing rain. Sunny, watching from the poui tree, was astonished to see his father standing motionless in the downpour. He had taken off his shirt, and his bare back and chest were shining with water. His face, uplifted to the sky, was the face of a man half-crazy with joy. He might be laughing or crying, Sunny could not tell; and his cheeks were streaming, perhaps with tears, perhaps with Parjanya's rain.

London

Gussy and the Boss

The organisation known as Industrial Corporation was taken over shortly after the war by a group of European businessmen with interests in the West Indies, and renamed the New Enterprises Company, with a financial backing of £50,000. The new owners had the buildings renovated where they stood on the southern outskirts of Port of Spain, a short distance from the railway station.

While the buildings were being painted and the old office furniture replaced, none of the employees knew that the company had changed hands. They commented that it was high time the dilapidated offices were given a complete overhauling and they tried out the new chairs and desks and came to words over who should have the mahogany table and this cabinet and that typewriter.

When the buildings had a new face and they were just settling down with renewed ambitions and resolutions to keep the rooms as tidy as possible, Mr

Jones, the boss, called a staff meeting one evening and told them.

He said he was sorry he couldn't tell them before – some arrangement with the new owners – but that Industrial Corporation was going out of business. He said he had been hoping that at least part of the staff would be able to remain, but he was sorry, the matter was entirely out of his hands, and they all had to go.

There were ten natives working in the offices at the time, and there was a middle-aged caretaker called Gussy. Gussy had one leg. A shark had bitten off the other in the Gulf of Paria while he was out fishing with some friends.

The ten employees – four girl typists and six clerks – had never thought of joining a trade union, partly because they felt that trade unions were for the poor struggling labourers and they were not of that class, and partly because the thought had never entered their heads that such a situation might arise. As it was, they could do nothing but make vain threats and grumble; one chap went to a newspaper and told the editor the whole story and asked him to do something about it. The editor promised and next day a reporter interviewed Mr Jones, and the following morning a small news item appeared saying that Industrial Corporation had been taken over by a group of wealthy Europeans, and that there was no doubt that the colony would benefit as a result, because new industries would be opened.

After two weeks the ten workers had cleared out leaving only Mr Jones and Gussy. Gussy gathered his courage and spoke to Mr Jones.

He said: 'Boss, you know how long I here with the business. I is a poor man, boss, and I have a ailing mother to support, and I sure I can't get a work no-where else. Please chief, you can't talk to the new bosses and them, and put in a good word for this poor one-legged man, and ask them to keep me? I ain't have a big work, is just to stay in the back of the place and see that nobody interfere with anything. Make a try for me please, pusher, the Good Lord will reward you in due course, and I would appreciate it very much.'

Mr Jones heard Gussy mumble through this long speech and he promised to see what he could do, grateful that the caretaker had given him the opportunity to make peace in his own mind, thinking that Gussy's salvation would absolve him from responsibility for the sacking of the others.

A week later the new staff arrived. Gussy hid behind a door in the storeroom and peeped between a crack because he was afraid to face all the new people at once. His agitation increased greatly as he saw that they were all white people. Were they all bosses then? The women too?

Later in the morning, while he was sweeping out the storeroom as noiselessly as possible, one of the new employees came to him.

'You're Gussy, the caretaker?' he asked in a kind voice.

Gussy dropped the broom and shoved his crutch under his arm quickly, standing up like a soldier at attention.

'Yes boss, I is the caretaker.'

'Mr Blade would like a word with you. He is the new manager, as you probably know.'

'What about, sir? My job is the caretaker job. My name is Gussy. I lives in Belmont. Age forty-five. No children. I lives with my mother. I gets pay every Friday . . .'

'I know all that,' the young man smiled a little. 'I am in charge of the staff we have here now. But Mr Blade wants to see you. Just for a little chat, he likes to be personally acquainted with everyone who works for him.'

Gussy's eyes opened wide and showed white. 'So I still have the job, chief? You all not going to fire me?'

'Of course not! Come along, Mr Blade is a busy man.'

When he returned to his post at the back of the building a few minutes later Gussy was full of praise for the new boss, mumbling to himself because there was no one to talk with. When he went home in the evening he told his mother:

'You can't imagine! He is a nice man, he even nicer than Mr Jones! He tell me is all right, that I could stay on the job as the caretaker, being as I was here so long already. When I tell you the man nice!'

But as the days went by Gussy wasn't happy at his job any more. He couldn't get accustomed to the idea that white people were working all around him. He treated everyone as he treated Mr Blade, stumping along as swiftly as he could to open the garage door or fill the water cooler or do whatever odd chore he was called upon to perform. In the old days he was in the habit of popping in and out of the outer office, sharing a word here and a joke there with the native workers. But now, he kept strictly to the back of the building, turning out an hour earlier to clean out the offices before any of the staff arrived. True, they treated him friendly, but Gussy couldn't get rid of the idea that they were all bosses.

After a week of loneliness he ventured near to the office door and peeped inside to see how the white people were working.

The young man who had spoken to him the first day, Mr Garry, saw him and called him inside.

Gussy stumped over to his desk with excuses.

'I was only looking to see if everything all right, boss, to see if anybody want anything, the weather hot, I could go and get some ice outside for you right now . . .'

Garry said: 'It's all right, Gussy, and I don't mind you coming to the office now and then.' He lowered his voice. 'But you watch out for the boss's wife. Sometimes she drops in unexpectedly to see him, and it wouldn't do for her to see you out here, because . . . well, because here is not the place you're supposed to be, you understand?'

'But sure boss, Mr Garry, I won't come back here

again, not at all at all unless you send for me, I promise you that boss, sure, sure . . .'

Whenever Mr Blade drove up in his Buick Eight, Gussy was there with a rag to wipe the car.

'You know, Gussy,' Mr Blade told him one morning, 'you manage to do more with that one leg of yours than many a normal man I know.'

'Thank you very much respectfully and gratefully, boss sir, all the offices clean, the water cooler full up, all the ink pots full up, the storeroom pack away just as Mr Garry want it . . .'

One evening when he had opened the garage door for the boss and he was reversing out – with Gussy standing at the back and giving all sorts of superfluous directions with his crutch which Mr Blade ignored – the boss looked out of the car window and said:

'By the way, Gussy, how much do you work for?'

'Ten dollars a week chief sir, respectfully, it not very much, with me minding my poor mother, but is enough, sir, I can even manage on less than that if you feel that it too much . . .'

'I was thinking of giving you more, what with the rising cost of living. Let me see, today is Wednesday.

Come to see me on Friday morning and we'll talk about it.'

Mr Blade drove off with Gussy's effusive thanks just warming up.

The next afternoon was hot, and Gussy was feeling drowsy as he sat on a soapbox in the storeroom. He felt a strong temptation to go and stand near the office door. The knowledge that he was soon going to earn a bigger salary gave him courage. He got up and went and positioned himself just outside the door.

He was just in time to hear Mr Garry telling the others about how his plane was shot down during the war, and Gussy listened wide-eyed.

Gussy heard a step behind him and turned around. He didn't know it was the boss's wife, but it wouldn't have made any difference, he would have behaved the same way with any white person.

'Just looking in to see if the bosses and them want anything at all no offence madam indeed . . .'

This time he dropped the crutch in his consternation.

The woman gave him a withering look and swept past the outer office.

Mr Blade was sitting in his swivel chair, facing the sea. It was a hot afternoon and he had the window fully opened, but the wind that came in was heavy and lifeless, as if the heat had taken all the spirit out of it.

Mr Blade was a kindly man newly arrived in the colony from England. He was also a weak man, and he knew it. Sometimes Blade was afraid of life because he was weak and couldn't make decisions or face up to facts and circumstances. The palms of his hands were always wet when he was excited or couldn't find the answer to a problem.

As he sat and watched the sea sparkle, he was thinking in a general sort of way about his life, and when his wife burst into the office he started.

'Oh hello, dear, didn't expect to see you today.'

Whenever Blade looked at his wife he saw the symbol of his weakness. All his faults were magnified and concentrated on her face, which was like a mirror in which he looked and shrank.

'Herbert.' She also had a most disquieting habit of getting to the point right away. 'I thought you had dismissed all the natives who were here before we came?'

'Of course, dear. As you can see, we only have Europeans and one or two whites who were born in the island.'

'I met a dirty one-legged man outside the office just as I was coming in – who's he?'

'Oh heavens, he's only the caretaker! Surely you didn't think he was on the staff?' Blade shifted his eyes and looked at an almanac on the wall above his wife's head.

'You'll have to get rid of him, you know.'

When she finished speaking, he knew that those last words would stay long after she left, from the tone in which she spoke. All their conversations were like that – everything else forgotten but the few words she spoke in that tone. He had got into the habit of listening for it. She had a special way of summing up, of finalising matters. He knew, from that moment – in a quick panic of fear which brought the sweat out on his palms – that the caretaker would have to go.

'Let's don't argue about it now, dear. I don't feel very well in this damned heat.'

And the next morning Blade sat down in the swivel chair and he faced the sea again. He knew he was going to fire Gussy, but he tried to think that he wasn't. He wiped the palms of his hands with a white handkerchief. All his life it had been like that; he felt the old fear of uncertainty and instability which had driven him from England return, and he licked his lips nervously.

He swung the chair and looked at the almanac on the wall. He addressed it as if it were his wife.

'That's a silly attitude to adopt,' he said to the almanac in a firm voice. 'You can't do that sort of thing. On the contrary, it is a good prestige for the place that we have a coloured worker. I think we should have more – after all, they do the work just as well.'

He sneered at the almanac, then looked for some other object in the room to represent Gussy. He fixed his eyes on the out-basket on his desk.

'The way how things are at present,' he told the basket, 'I'm afraid you'll have to go. We don't really need a caretaker any more, and we can always get a woman to come in and clean the offices. I personally didn't have anything to do with it, mind you, it was . . . er, the decision of the directors. I am sorry to lose you, Gussy, you are a hard, honest worker.'

For a minute Blade wondered if there wasn't something he could do – post money secretly to the man every week, or maybe give him a tidy sum to tide him over for a few months.

The next minute he was laughing mirthlessly – once the handkerchief fell and he unconsciously rubbed his hands together and he heard the squelching sound made by the perspiration. And he talked and reasoned with all the objects in the room, as if they were companions, and some objects agreed and others didn't.

The pencil and the inkpot said it was all right, he was a fool to worry, why didn't he get Garry to do the dirty work, and the almanac told him to get it over with quickly for Christ's sake, but the window and the wall and the telephone said Gussy was a poor, harmless creature and he, Blade, was a spineless, unprincipled dog, who didn't know his own mind and wasn't fit to live.

With an impatient, indecisive gesture Blade jabbed the button on his desk. One of the girls opened the door.

'That caretaker we have – what is his name – Gusher or Gully or something like that' – the lie in his deliberate lapse of memory stabbed him – 'send him in to see me, will you, please.'

Gussy was waiting to be called. He had told Mr Garry how the boss would be wanting to see him, and that was why he was keeping so near to the office, so they wouldn't have any trouble finding him.

Gussy didn't have any idea how much more money he was going to get, but whatever it was, first thing he was going to do was buy a bottle of polish and shine down the boss's car to surprise him. After that, anything could happen.

He stood in a corner, quietly calculating on his fingers how much he would have to pay if he wanted to put down three months' rent in advance.

'Oh, there you are, Gussy,' the girl caught sight of him as she came out. 'Mr Blade wants to see you. You'd better go in right away.'

'Thank you madam, I am right here, going in to see the boss right away, with all due respects, no delay at all.'

Gussy shoved his crutch under his armpit and stumped as softly as he could to the boss's door.

Calypso in London

One winter a kind of blight fall on Mangohead in London. As if he can't make a note nohow, no matter where he turn. Not only he can't get a work nowhere, but he can't even pick up a little thing to keep company with, nor bounce a borrow from any of the boys, nor even get a pleasant good morning from the landlady.

Mangohead sit down in his room to ponder on the situation. Mangohead come from St Vincent, and if you don't know where that is that is your hard luck. But I will give you a clue – he uses to work on a arrowroot plantation. Now I suppose you want to know what arrowroot is, eh?

Mangohead had a sharp work in the summer. You ever notice sometimes, when you hustling to the office, that it have four-five fellars stand up or sit down around a hole in the pavement, and one fellar inside the hole as if he fixing some kind of electric cable, with half a cigarette in his mouth? Well Mangohead had a work, where he was one of the four-five fellars who sitting around.

Things was all right until it start to get cold. They was digging up the road in Hampstead to lay cable, and it was so cold poor Mangohead was shivering. And them other English fellars giving him tone, asking him if he wouldn't like to be in the tropics right now, and saying: 'Too cold for you mate?' and winking and nudging one another when Mangohead stand up near the wood fire that they light on the pavement to keep warm.

Well Mangohead try hard with the work, bearing the cold. Then one frosty morning when he was digging, he lift up a spadeful of dirt to throw up on the bank, and when he throw his hands over his shoulder, as if his hands catch cramp and couldn't come back. Mangohead hands stay like that, as if they get frozen in that position, and all he try he couldn't move his hands. At last, by turning his body a little, he manage to get the hands a little lower, and he drop the spade.

Mangohead climb up out of the trench, went and wash his hands, and tell the foreman that he finish with the work.

He thought it would of been easy to get another

work, somewhere out of the cold. But the blight start from the day he leave the trench.

Mangohead comb all the factories and canteens, and he ask the boys about vacancies, but nothing was doing.

One morning he get a wire that a cigarette factory in the East End was taking fellars, and he hustle and went, but when he get there the fellar say sorry, no vacancies. This time so, I don't have to tell you how the winter grim in London – I mean, I don't think it have any other place in the world where the weather so powerful, and Mangohead drifting through the fog and the smog and snow getting in his shoes and the wind passing right through him as if he ain't have on any clothes at all.

Well Mango had a friend in the East End, name Hotboy, who was a fellar from Trinidad what used to compose calypso. Hotboy have a mysterious way of living. All day long he sitting in a Indian tailor shop in Cable Street, talking politics, or else harking back to the old days in Trinidad, because the Indian fellar who own the shop name Rahamut and he also come from Trinidad. Sometimes Hotboy in some real old talk about them days back home, telling Rahamut about how he was one of the best calypsonians it had in Trinidad, how he compose numbers like 'I Saw You Doing It Last Night' and 'That Is A Thing I Could Do Anytime, Anywhere'. Well Hotboy always saying about how he would make a comeback one day, how he would compose a calypso that would be hearts, and it would sell plenty and he would make money and come rich.

All these things Mangohead remember when he get turn away from the cigarette factory, and he start to make a bee for the tailor shop, hoping to make a little borrow from Hotboy, something like ten shillings, or if not, five, or if not, a two and six, or if not at least a cuppa, old man. Also, Mangohead suddenly feeling creative. As if all the troubles he in put him in a thoughtful mood, and while he meditating on the downs of life, he feel like composing a calypso that would tell everybody how life treating him.

> It had a time in this country
> When everybody happy excepting me
> I can't get a work no matter how I try
> It look as if hard times riding me high.

This was not the first time Mangohead get vap to create calypso: many times before Hotboy drive him away when he go to him with some sharp ideas, but Mangohead feel that this is it, that this time he really have something, that Hotboy sure to like the words and set up a tune for them.

When he get to the tailor shop, Hotboy in a hot debate with Rahamut about the Suez issue. 'If I was Nasser . . .' Hot was saying, and going on to say what and what he wouldn't do.

Now, from the time Hot see Mango, he stop talking about the Suez Canal, and before poor Mango could say anything Hot say:

'Yes, I know what you come round here for, since you borrow ten shillings from me last week you lose the address, and you only come now to tell me that you expecting a work next week, and if I could lend you another ten please God until you start to work. But Mangohead you lie, you hear? I telling you in front, no, no, no. I ain't lending you a nail till you pay me back that ten.'

'But look at my crosses!' Mango rise to the occasion fast. '*Me* borrow money from you! That was the last thing in my mind! You so bad-minded you can't feel that I just come to pay a social visit?'

But Hot cagey, he only grunting and eyeing Mango

suspiciously, as if he still expect Mango to plead for a borrow.

Mango say: 'Hotboy, I have an idea here for a calypso that is hearts. I sure when you hear it you will agree, and set up a tune for it. We might even get it play by the BBC.'

Now Hot tired asking Mango to leave calypso alone, telling him that that is not his line. Time and again he chase Mango when Mango come with some stupid words, saying that the words would make a firstclass calypso.

'But Mango, who tell you you could write calypso? When you was in Trinidad you only used to work drilling oil in Point-à-Pierre. How much time I have to tell you to leave calypso alone?'

'But man Hotboy, I sure this time! I have some words here that would kill people when they hear.'

Hotboy get up off the cardboard carton he was sitting on: same time Rahamut see the carton break up how Hotboy was sitting on it and he say: 'Look what the hell you do with the box, I tell you not to sit down on it.'

But Hotboy ignore him, and turn to Mango again: 'You sure you don't want to borrow money?'

Mango make the sign of the cross with his fore-fingers and kiss it.

'All right,' Hotboy say grudgingly, 'let we go in the back of the shop.'

So they went in the back of the shop, which part Rahamut have a table and two chairs, and they sit down there and Hotboy tell Mango: 'Let me hear these brave words.'

So Mango begin, but from the time he begin Hotboy chock his ears with his fingers and bawl out: 'Lord old man, you can't think of anything new? You think we still in Trinidad? This is London, man, this is London. The people want calypso on topical subject.'

'That is only the first verse,' Mango say, 'I am coming to the Suez issue.'

And Mango, as if he get an inspiration, start to extemporise on Nasser and Eden and how he will give them the dope – the best thing is to pass the ships round the Cape of Good Hope.

'Like you have something there,' Hotboy concede, and he begin to hum a little tune.

Well in fifteen minutes' time, in that tailor shop in the East End, the two boys had a calypso shaping up, and it wasn't a bad number, either.

Rahamut and the English assistant he have come and stand up listening, and when the calypso finish singing the English fellar say: 'That is one of the best calypsos I ever heard.'

But Rahamut say: 'Why you don't shut your mouth? What you English people know about calypso?'

'Well Rahamut what you think of it, eh?' Mango ask.

Rahamut want to say yes, it good, but he beating about the bush, he hemming and he hawing, he saying: 'Well, it so-so,' and 'It not so bad,' and 'I hear a lot of worse ones.'

But the English fellar who does assist Rahamut, he like the tune too bad, he only slapping Mango and Hotboy on the back and saying how he never hear a calypso like that. He swinging his hands in the air while he talking, and his hand hit Rahamut hand and Rahamut get a prick with a needle he was holding.

Well Rahamut put the finger in his mouth and suck it, and he turn round and start to abuse the English fellar, asking him if he don't know people does get blood poisoning with needle prick.

Hotboy really impressed with the words Mango

think up, and he begin to have dreams again about a comeback: he could hear this calypso playing all about in London, and people going wild when they hear it.

And as if he could read Hotboy mind, Mango realise that it was now or never if he going to tap Hotboy, so he turn to him and say softly: 'Hotboy, things really hard with me these days, you know. Why you don't lend me another ten, and make it a pound I have for you?'

Hotboy have a piece of paper before him and he writing down the calypso and concentrating hard on it: he tell Mango, 'Yes, yes,' not even realising what it is that Mango say.

'You hear that Rahamut?' Mango say quickly. 'You give me the ten, as Hotboy busy with the calypso, and afterwards he will fix you up.'

'I don't believe Hotboy hear what you say at all,' Rahamut cagey.

'You didn't hear for yourself?' Mango begin to push Rahamut and the English fellar out of the backroom. 'Leave him alone to concentrate on the number, don't interrupt him at all.'

In the front of the tailor shop big argument start up between Mango and Rahamut. Rahamut saying he sure that Hotboy didn't hear what Mango say, and Mango asking Rahamut if he deaf, if he didn't hear Hotboy say yes, yes.

In the end Mango manage to get the ten from Rahamut and he peel off fast, to hustle a cuppa and a hot pie.

About half an hour later Hotboy come to the front of the shop and ask: 'Which part Mango gone?'

'Mango gone,' Rahamut say, 'and I give him ten shillings for you. You better give it to me now before you forget.'

'Mango gone!' Hotboy repeat. 'You give him ten shillings for me! What you talking about?'

'John,' Rahamut turn to the English fellar, 'you didn't witness everything?'

But the English fellar start to get on cagey too, he see this sort of thing happening plenty times before and he don't want to become involved in any arguments the boys have.

'I was busy,' he say, and he went on sewing.

All the argue Rahamut argue Hotboy won't give him the ten. And that is as much as I know of the ballad. The other evening, liming in Marble Arch, I bounce up with Mango and he tell me that he went to see Hotboy and Hotboy tell him that he sell the calypso.

But up to now I can't hear it playing or singing anywhere, though I sure the number was really hearts, and would make some money for the boys if it catch on and sell.

Eraser's Dilemma

If you are one of the hustlers on Route 12 I don't know how you could fail to notice Eraser, he such a cheerful conductor. And if you look good, under the regulation uniform, you might notice him wearing a happy nylon shirt, green, with red stripes.

That shirt is Eraser's pet wear, and if you have a bus fare and want to take a ride – in fact, the beauty is you might be on his bus now even as you reading this – I will give you the ballad about that happy shirt.

To Londoners a bus is a bus. If you queueing for one and another come along, you just hop in, as long as it take you where you want to go. The red double-deckers come as nothing, a sight you seeing day in and day out.

Eraser had a different feeling about them. Like how a sailor love his ship, so Eraser love his bus, and it hurt him to go off duty and hand over to another conductor who mightn't feel the way he do. Seeing that he couldn't be sure of always working the same bus, Eraser adopt the route and determine to make it the nicest one in London.

And in point of fact, though I wouldn't say that one man able to work a route smoothly or even one bus on the route for that matter, it is true that from the time Eraser begin to work on Route 12, a change for the better take place.

One or two letter even appear in the newspaper complimenting L.T. on the improvement, and once a lady that was helped on and off a bus write to say how wonderful these West Indians were, that she notice they was extremely kind and polite and did their job well. (I only telling you what the lady say.)

Them kind of letter, you don't see them often, but whenever one appear concerning his route Eraser keep the clipping to send home to St Vincent to his grandmother.

Once he send a photo of the bus he working on. He take it out in the garage, with him hugging the bonnet like how you see them jockeys holding on to the horse neck when they come in first, and he send the photo home.

You should hear them in St Vincent, talking about it, wanting to know why the bus so high, and why it have upstairs and downstairs.

Well, when Eraser on duty, it ain't have nothing like woman standing in his bus at all. From the time that begin to happen Eraser saying out loud: 'Which gallant Englishman will give this lady his seat?'

I don't have to tell you what happen when Eraser say that. Everybody get quiet as if they in church. A test working in the City, with bowler and brolly, bury his face in the *Financial Times*. Some fellars looking out the window and admiring the London scenery. Other fellars as if they deaf.

'Come now,' you should hear Eraser, 'surely there are gentlemen on my bus?'

And eventually one or two fellars would get up, glaring at Eraser, and all the women in the bus would look at him and smile among themselves.

Well, it had one of these old ladies what used to catch Eraser bus as regular as clockwork, and he always there to help her on and off. And they would exchange the usual about the weather, and how are you today, and that sort of thing, and if trade not very busy she would tell Eraser to sing a calypso, and he would oblige, because he is that sort of fellar. I mean, all the time he working he whistling or singing, spreading sunshine in the bus. Nothing could dampen the old Eraser.

What happen one day is this. The old lady get on the bus with a parcel, but when she get off she forget to take it. Other passengers see the parcel, but you know how it is in London, everybody lock-up and suspicious, nobody ain't say a word.

Eraser decide to keep the parcel instead of handing it in at the garage, feeling it would be nice to give it to her himself the next day when she catch the bus, and save her the trouble of going quite to Baker Street to the Lost Property Office.

He tell Jack, the driver, who was a steady, unimaginative fellar about it. Jack just shrug and say if he wanted to take the chance it was his business.

Well the next day when the bus get to the stop where the old lady uses to get on, no old lady there. Eraser get uneasy. These English people, they have habits, and Eraser know she would wait for his bus as she always did all the months he on the route.

He went home worried, but thinking he would see she the next day.

Next day come. No old lady.

Eraser went to Jack when they was having a break for tea at the garage.

'You remember that parcel,' Eraser say. 'Well, the old lady ain't turn up since.'

'Do you know her name?' Jack ask.

'No,' Eraser say.

'Isn't there any address on the parcel?' Jack ask.

'No,' Eraser say.

'You should have handed it in the first day,' Jack say.

'I will wait one more day, maybe she is sick,' Eraser say.

Jack shrug and went on with his elevenses.

Well the third day come. By the bus stop, no old lady.

Eraser begin to sweat. He even allow a lady to stand up for five minutes before he realise she should be sitting instead of one of the hulky fellars in the bus. Just because he wanted to do a good turn, it look like trouble catch up with him.

Eraser get off duty at twelve o'clock and didn't even bother about lunch. He went to the bus stop which part the old lady uses to wait. At this stage the parcel like live coal in his hand, and he praying that he would meet somebody who know her.

But three-four people that he stop and ask, none of them know who he mean.

'It can't be far from here,' Eraser say to himself, combing the district around the bus-stop.

And this time, he imagining all sorts of things, how L.T. would want to know why he didn't turn in the parcel, if he didn't know the rules and regulations. They might even think he wanted to thief the parcel. What he would say to all that?

And so he in this panic as he searching, because he like his job and things was going all right until this had to happen.

At last, in a small sweet-shop, he strike some luck. Yes, the attendant think she know who he talking about, an old lady called Miss Bellflent, living at No. 5.

Eraser take off in this street looking for No. 5, and he ring all the buzzers it had on the door when he get there. He could hardly ask the landlady for Miss Bellflent when she come to the door.

'Miss Bellflent?' the landlady say. 'Why, she left a few days ago. She isn't staying here any more.'

Eraser see himself in big trouble, out of a job, no bus to conduct.

'Do you know where she lives now?' he ask weakly.

'No.'

In his mind Eraser begin taking off his uniform for the last time. Things always hard on the boys, and now he was having his share. He could imagine what everybody would be saying, oh yes they are cheerful and work well, but after all . . .

And the landlady, as if she could see how important it was, and noticing the disappointment on Eraser's face, say: 'Wait a minute,' and she went inside.

When she come back she give Eraser a address on a piece of paper. 'Try there,' she said. Eraser was making up the road before he remember to turn round and shout: 'Thank you!'

At last it look like there was still hope, and he race to the address, and when he knock and Miss Bellflent open the door, he feel to kiss her.

'Why, it's you!' Miss Bellflent say. 'Do come in!'

And when Eraser get inside, she tell him to sit down and she put the tea-kettle on the fire right away.

'You must have a cup of tea,' she said kindly.

'I only came about this parcel which you forgot

on the bus.' Eraser say, throwing the world off his shoulders, and putting down the parcel on the table and wiping his hands, as if he too glad it was finish with.

'But I meant it for you!' Miss Bellflent say in a matter-of-fact way. 'I thought I wrote a note on the box. How absent-minded of me.'

'For me?' Eraser stand up by the table as if he stun.

'Yes, of course!' Miss Bellflent say, pouring out the tea. 'Go on then, aren't you going to open it?'

Eraser touch the parcel as if he frighten. He loosen the string and open a box.

Inside, it had a happy nylon shirt, green, with red stripes.

Brackley and the Bed

One evening Brackley was cruising round by the Embankment looking for a soft bench to rest his weary bones, and to cogitate on the ways of life. The reason for that, and the reason why the boys begin to call him Rockabye, you will find out as the ballad goes on.

Brackley hail from Tobago, which part they have it to say Robinson Crusoe used to hang out with Man Friday. Things was brown in that island and he make for England and manage to get a work and was just settling down when bam! he get a letter from his aunt saying that Teena want to come England too.

Teena was Brackley distant cousin and they was good friends in Tobago. In fact, the other reason why Brackley hustle from the island is because it did look like he and Teena was heading for a little married thing, and Brackley run.

Well, right away he write aunty and say no, no, because he have a feeling this girl would make botheration if she come England. The aunt write back to say she didn't mean to say that Teena want to come England, but that Teena left Tobago for England already.

Brackley hold his head and bawl. And the evening the boat train come in at Waterloo, he went there and start 'busing she right away not waiting to ask how the folks at home was or anything.

'What you doing in London?' Brackley ask as soon as Teena step off the train. 'What you come here for, eh? Even though I write home to say things real hard?'

'What happen, you buy the country already?' Teena sheself giving tit for tat right away. 'You ruling England now? The Queen abdicate?'

'You know where you going?' Brackley say. 'You know where you is? You know what you going to do?'

'I am going straight to the Colonial Office,' Teena say.

'What you think the Colonial Office is, eh? You think they will do anything for you? You have a god-father working there?'

Well, they argue until in the end Brackley find himself holding on to Teena suitcase and they on the way to the little batchy he have in Golders Green at the time.

When they get there Teena take one look at the room and sniff. 'But look at the state you have this room in! You ain't ashamed of yourself?'

'Listen,' Brackley say, 'you better don't let me and you have contention. I know this would of happen when you come.'

Teena start squaring up the room brisk-brisk.

'It making cold,' she say, putting chair this way and table that way and turning everything upside down for poor Brackley. 'How you does keep warm? Where the gas fire I hear so much about?'

Brackley grudgingly put a shilling in the meter and light the gas.

'What you have to eat?' But even as she asking she gone in the cupboard and begin pulling out rations that Brackley had stow away to see him through the winter. Brackley as if he mesmerise, stand up there watching her as she start up a peas and rice on the gas ring.

'You better go easy with them rations,' he say. 'I

not working now and money don't grow on tree here as in Tobago.'

When they was eating Teena say: 'Well you have to get a job right away. You was always a lazy fellar.'

'Keep quiet,' Brackley say, enjoying the meal that Teena cook in real West Indian fashion – the first good meal he ever had in London. 'You don't know nothing.'

'First thing tomorrow morning,' Teena say. 'What time you get up?'

'About nine – ten,' Brackley say vaguely.

'Well is six o'clock tomorrow morning, bright and early as the cock crow.'

'You don't hear cock crowing in London,' Brackley say. Then he drop the spoon he was eating with. 'Six o'clock! You must be mad! Six o'clock like midnight in the winter, and people still sound asleep.'

'Six o'clock,' Teena say.

Brackley finish eating and begin to smoke, whistling a calypso softly, as if he in another world and not aware of Teena at all.

'Ah well,' he say, stretching by the fire, 'that wasn't a bad meal. Look, I will give you some old blankets

and you could wrap up that coat and use as a pillow –
you could sleep on the ground in that corner . . .'

'*Me*? On the floor? You not ashamed?'

'Well, is only one bed here as you see . . .'

'I using the bed.'

'Girl, is winter, and if you think I going to sleep in
the corner with two old blanket and wake up stiff . . .'

But, in the end, was Brackley who crouch up in
the corner, and Teena sound asleep in the bed.

It look to Brackley like he hardly shut his eyes
before Teena was shaking him.

'Get up,' Teena say, 'six o'clock.'

Brackley start to curse.

'None of that,' Teena say. 'No bad language when
I around.'

Teena move around fast and give Brackley breakfast and make him dress and get out on the cold
streets mumbling, 'Get a job, get a job,' before he
knew what happening.

It was only about 10 o'clock, when he was washing
dishes in a café where he get a work, that Brackley
realise what was happening to him.

When he get home in the evening, Teena have
screen put up around the bed and everything spick

and span, and Brackley don't know where to look even for chair to sit down.

'I see you make yourself at home,' he say maliciously.

'And what you think?' Teena flares.

'The boys does come here sometimes for a little rummy.'

'None of that now.'

'And sometimes a girl-friend visit me.'

'None of that now.'

'So you taking over completely.'

'Aunty say to look after you.'

'Why the hell you come England, eh?'

Well, a pattern begin to form as the weeks go by, but the main thing that have Brackley worried is the bed. Every night he curl up in the corner shivering, and by the time he doze off: 'Six o'clock, get up, you have to go to work.'

Brackley ain't sleep on bed for weeks. The thing like an obsession with him. He window-shopping on the way home and looking at them bed and soft mattress on show and closing his eyes and sighing. Single divan, double divan, put-you-up, put-you-down – all makes and sizes he looking at.

One night when frost was forming on the window pane Brackley wake up and find he couldn't move.

'Teena.'

'What?'

'You sleeping?'

'Yes.'

'Teena, you want to get married?'

'Married? To who?'

'To me.'

'What for?'

'So I could sleep in the bed– I mean, well, we uses to know one another good in Tobago, and now that you here in London, what you think?'

'Well, all right, but you have to change your ways.'

'Yes, Teena.'

'And no foolishness when we married. You come home straight from work. And I don't want you looking at no white girls.'

'Yes, Teena.'

No sooner said than done. Brackley hustle Teena off to the registry office as soon as things was fixed, thinking only how nice the bed would be after the hard floor and the cold, with Teena to help keep him warm.

'What about honeymoon?' Teena say after the ceremony.

'In the summer,' Brackley say. 'Let we go home. I am tired and I feel I could sleep for weeks.'

'Bracks,' Teena say as they was coming away, 'I have a nice surprise for you. Guess who coming to London this evening?'

'Father Christmas,' Brackley says yawning.

'No. Aunty. I write telling her to come up, as the room not so small and we could manage until we get another place. And then she and me could get a work too, and that will help.'

'You putting hell 'pon jackass back,' Brackley moan. But it was only when they reach home that a great fear come to Brackley. He had was to sit down in a chair before he could talk.

'But Teena,' he say quietly, 'we ain't have no place for Aunty to sleep.'

'Don't worry,' Teena say, 'She can sleep with me until we find another place.'

If Winter Comes

It does have certain times in London, when a kind of blight descend on the boys. Everybody hard-up, and you can't get a ease-up from your best friend. And the point is, it don't happen in summer, when at least you have a little sunshine and a daffodil or tulip to console you, but in them grim days of winter when night fall on the city from three o'clock in the afternoon, and you looking all about in the fog for a friend to borrow a shilling for the gas meter.

But everybody cagey-cagey, men looking at you with suspicion from the time you appear in the distance, and some fellars, as if they have radar, could sense when a hard-up test on the horizon, and right away they begin to limp and cry big water, so that by the time you get near you realise it have a situation here that far worse than yours.

I mean, when a fellar like Brakes can't manage a borrow, you could imagine what the situation like. Because Brakes have a way, he would mamaguile you with all kind of sweet-talk, and hark back to the old days in the islands, and when he have the memories well-stirred, of a sudden he would come out with something like: 'Lend me four shillings and five-pence ha'penny, boy – I in a jam.'

Notice the sum he ask for: When Brakes making a tap he always asking for a particular sum as if he have something direct in mind.

But no approach was successful that season.

'These look like evil days,' Brakes say to himself. 'What happen to everybody? I will have to think of something.'

He had to put the old brains to work, because Mavis was after a coat that she see in a store in Oxford Street (the same place where Nina bounce some hats and cause havoc in international relationships) and this coat cost exactly £10. But as far as Brakes concern it might as well cost £500.

'Same reason I don't like to come window-shopping with you,' Brakes grumble. 'Everything you see you want.'

'I must have that coat, Brakes,' Mavis say, as if she didn't hear him at all.

'You know I ain't have a work now,' Brakes say.

'If you love me, you would get that coat for me, Brakes.'

Well I ain't fooling you, but woman really bad, *oui*. Mavis stick behind Brakes like a leech, until he had was to promise to get it for her before the next week out.

Brakes stand up by Tottenham Court Tube station pondering the situation when she left him. And the only thing he could think of, is to get some fellars to take a hand in a sou-sou. That is a thing like this: about ten of you decide to give a pound each every week, and the £10 would make the rounds of each person, and at the end of the ten weeks each one will have had £10.

But Brakes figuring on running a sou-sou where he don't have to put anything in. He planning to get ten fellars beside himself, and don't tell them is really eleven and not ten. And naturally he takes the first £10 collected for himself. After that things would go all right until it come to the last week, when two fellars would be expecting to collect, 'and by that time something bound to turn up,' Brakes tell himself.

Well, he get eight of the boys and two English fellars, and he went around like a landlord the first payday and collect the ten, and right after went and buy the coat for Mavis.

Mavis put on the coat and want to go West End right away. They cruise round by the Dilly, but everytime Mavis stop by a show window Brakes pull she away before she could say she want this and she want that.

'We haven't been to the theatre a long time,' Mavis observe, wanting to show off the new coat.

'The most you getting is a walk in Trafalgar Square,' Brakes say, feeling in his pockets and only clutching air, 'to watch the fountains spouting water.'

Well the weeks breeze by, and two days was to go for the last two fellars in the sou-sou to get the money, and Brakes wasn't nearer a work, much less the money.

He dress and went out in the last act of despair the boys resort to – looking for money in the streets. You don't know sometimes what your luck might be – you might spot a crumple-up pound note or a ten shilling somewhere on the pavement where people walking so fast that they ain't have time to look down.

Brakes have time – in fact his face rivet-down to

the ground, but he reach to them side streets in Soho and the most he find is two safety pin. That wasn't a happy hunting ground, because it have a lot of tests does be liming there and if anybody drop a note or even a tanner by accident, you could be sure it hardly have time settle on the ground before a test ups it.

But Brakes wasn't thinking where he going. He collide-up with a fellar who was in a hurry.

'What is all the rush, Chippy?' Brakes say, recognising a shady Englisher who live by gambling.

'I am on something hot,' Chippy say. 'I am off to put money on a sure horse.'

Brakes brain start to work tick-tock. 'What is the odds?' he ask Chippy.

'The odds are ten to one,' Chippy say. He make to move off, then he stop. 'Would you like me to put something on for you?' He pull Brakes to one side and talking in a whisper. 'Meet me here by three o'clock if you are interested.' And with that he takes off.

Well, by three o'clock Brakes hand Chippy a pound and remain sweating until the race finish. Praise the Lord, the horse come in and Brakes see his worries over for the time being. All he had to do was collect the last hand and then pay off the two fellars.

The last man in the sou-sou was a Englisher, and as soon as he see Brakes he say: 'Something fishy seems to be going on. I understand that this sou-sou thing is finished, and I haven't had any money. I have been looking all over town for you.'

'Take it easy,' Brakes say. 'I have the money right here for you.'

The Englisher lick his thumb and count the money. 'It was a good experience,' he say, 'but count me out the next time.'

After that, the only worry was Mavis. Brakes take a trip to the nearest public library and spent some time reading poetry before he went to pick her up after work.

'Did you manage to borrow money for the sousou?' was the first thing she ask him, because Brakes did tell her everything but she couldn't help.

'I bet on a horse and it come in,' Brakes say.

'Where did you get the money to bet?'

'Well,' Brakes start to fidget. 'I had to get this money somehow. Anyway, don't worry.' Brakes trying hard to remember the poetry he read in the library. 'You know that nice poetry about if winter come, spring running a close second. It only have a few more weeks and then no more winter, and people won't need to put on any heavy clothes.'

'What is all that in aid of?' Mavis suspicious and pull Brakes to one side of the pavement and stand up.

'Well, you won't need that coat any more,' Brakes say. 'I tell you, spring is just around the corner.'

'What are you trying to say?' Mavis say impatiently.

'I sell the coat for a pound to get money to bet. It's quite mild now, you don't think?'

Though the day was really mild Mavis start to shiver as if she have ague.

'Sold my coat!' she say, holding on to her shoulders and trembling with imaginary cold. 'Why did you do that, Brakes?'

'I keep telling you about the poetry that say if winter come, spring racing a close second. Only a few more days and . . .'

Mavis ready to cry. 'I haven't had a new coat for years. What will I do when winter comes again?'

Brakes ponder the question for a moment.

'Don't worry,' he say brightly. 'I will run another sou-sou and buy one for you!'

The Cricket Match

The time when the West Indies cricket eleven come to England to show the Englishmen the finer points of the game, Algernon was working in a tyre factory down by Chiswick way, and he lambast them English fellars for so.

'That is the way to play the game,' he tell them, as the series went on and West Indies making some big score and bowling out them English fellars for duck and thing, 'you thought we didn't know how to play the game, eh? That is cricket, lovely cricket.'

And all day he singing a calypso that he make up about the cricket matches that play, ending up by saying that in the world of sport, is to wait until the West Indies report.

Well in truth and in fact, the people in this country believe that everybody who come from the West Indies at least like the game even if they can't play it. But you could take it from me that it have some tests that don't like the game at all, and among them was Algernon. But he see a chance to give the Nordics tone and he get all the gen on the matches and players, and come like an authority in the factory on cricket. In fact, the more they ask him the more convinced Algernon get that perhaps he have the talent of a Walcott in him only waiting for a chance to come out.

They have a portable radio hide away from the foreman and they listening to the score every day. And as the match going on you should hear Algernon: 'Yes, lovely stroke,' and 'That should have been a six,' and so on. Meanwhile, he picking up any round object that near to hand and making demonstration, showing them how Ramadhin does spin the ball.

'I bet you used to play a lot back home,' the English fellars tell him.

'Who, me?' Algernon say. 'Man, cricket is breakfast and dinner where I come from. If you want to learn about the game you must go down there. I don't want to brag,' he say, hanging his head a little, 'but I used to live next door to Ramadhin, and we used to teach one another the fine points.'

But what you think Algernon know about cricket in truth? The most he ever play was in the street, with a bat make from a coconut branch, a dry mango seed for ball, and a pitchoil tin for wicket. And that was when he was a boy, and one day he get lash with the mango seed and since that time he never play again.

But all day long in the factory, he and another West Indian fellar name Roy getting on as if they invent the game, and the more the West Indies eleven score, the more they getting on. At last a Englisher name Charles, who was living in the suburbs, say to Algernon one morning:

'You chaps from the West Indies are really fine cricketers. I was just wondering . . . I play for a side where I live, and the other day I mentioned you and Roy to our captain, and he said why don't you organise an eleven and come down our way one Saturday for a match? Of course,' Charles went on earnestly, 'we don't expect to be good enough for you, but still, it will be fun.'

'Oh,' Algernon say airily, 'I don't know. I uses to play in first-class matches, and most of the boys I know accustom to a real good game with strong opposition. What kind of pitch you have?'

'The pitch is good,' Charles say. 'Real English turf.'

Algernon start to hedge. He scratch his head. He say, 'I don't know. What you think about the idea, Roy?'

Roy decide to hem and leave Algernon to get them out of the mooch. He say, 'I don't know, either. It sound like a good idea, though.'

'See what you can do,' Charles say, 'and let me know this week.'

Afterwards in the canteen having elevenses Roy tell Algernon: 'You see what your big mouth get us into.'

'*My* big mouth!' Algernon say. 'Who it is say he bowl four top bats for duck one after the other in a match in Queen's Park Oval in Port of Spain? Who it is say he score two hundred and fifty not out in a match against Jamaica?'

'Well to tell you the truth Algernon,' Roy say, now that they was down to brass tacks, 'I ain't play cricket for a long time. In fact, I don't believe I could still play.'

'Me too, boy,' Algernon say. 'I mean, up here in England you don't get a chance to practise or anything. I must be out of form.'

They sit down there in the canteen cogitating on the problem.

'Anyway,' Roy say, 'it look as if we will have to hustle an eleven somehow. We can't back out of it now.'

'I studying,' Algernon say, scratching his head. 'What about Eric, you think he will play?'

'You could ask him, he might. And what about Williams? And Wilky? And Heads? Those boys should know how to play.'

'Yes, but look at trouble to get them! Wilky working night and he will want to sleep. Heads is a man you can't find when you want. And Williams – I ain't see him for a long time, because he owe me a pound and he don't come my way these days.'

'Still,' Roy say, 'we will have to manage to get a side together. If we back out of this now them English fellars will say we are only talkers. You better wait for me after work this evening, and we will go around by some of the boys and see what we could do.'

That was the Monday, and the Wednesday night about twelve of the boys get together in Algernon room in Kensal Rise, and Algernon boiling water in the kettle and making tea while they discuss the situation.

'Algernon always have big mouth, and at last it land him in trouble.'

'Cricket! I never play in my life!'

'I uses to play a little "pass-out" in my days, but to go and play against a English side! Boy, them fellars like this game, and they could play, too!'

'One time I hit a ball and it went over a fence and break a lady window and . . .'

'All right, all right, ease up on the good old days, the problem is right now. I mean, we have to rally.'

'Yes, and then when we go there everybody get bowl for duck, and when them fellars batting we can't get them out. Not me.'

But in the end, after a lot of blague and argument, they agree that they would go and play.

'What about some practice?' Wilky say anxiously. Wilky was the only fellar who really serious about the game.

'Practice!' Roy say. 'I ain't have time for that. I wonder if I could still hold a bat?' And he get up and pick up a stick Algernon had in the corner and begin to make stance.

'Is not that way to hold a bat, stupid. Is so.'

And there in Algernon room the boys begin to

remember what they could of the game, and Wilky saying he ain't playing unless he is captain, and Eric saying he ain't playing unless he get pads because one time a cork ball nearly break his shinbone, and a fellar name Chips pull a cricket cap from his back pocket and trying it on in front a mirror.

So everything was arranged in a half-hearted sort of way. When the great day come, Algernon had hopes that they might postpone the match, because only eight of the boys turn up, but the English captain say it was a shame for them to return without playing, that he would make his side eight, too.

Well that Saturday on the village green was a historic day. Whether cold feet take the English side because of the licks the West Indies eleven was sharing at Lord's I can't say, but the fact is that they had to bowl first and they only coming down with some nice hop-and-drop that the boys lashing for six and four.

When Algernon turn to bat he walk out like a veteran. He bend down and inspect the pitch closely and shake his head, as if he ain't too satisfied with the condition of it but had to put up with it. He put on gloves, stretch out his hands as if he about to shift a heavy tyre in the factory, and take up the most unorthodox stance them English fellars ever did see. Algernon legs wide apart as if he doing the split and he have the bat already swing over his shoulder although the bowler ain't bowl yet. The umpire making sign to him that he covering the wicket but Algernon do as if he can't see. He make up his mind that he rather go for l.b.w. than for the stumps to fly.

No doubt an ordinary ball thrown with ease would have had him out in two-twos, but as I was saying, it look as if the unusual play of the boys have the Englishers in a quandary, and the bowler come down with a nice hop-and-drop that a baby couldn't miss.

Algernon close his eyes and he make a swipe at the ball, and he swipe so hard that when the bat collide the ball went right out of the field and fall in the road.

Them Englishers never see a stroke like that in their lives. All heads turn up to the sky watching the ball going.

Algernon feel like a king: only thing, when he hit the ball the bat went after it and nearly knock down a English fellar who was fielding silly-mid-on-square-leg.

Well praise the Lord, the score was then sixty-nine and one set of rain start to fall and stop the match.

Later on, entertaining the boys in the local pub, the Englishers asking all sort of questions, like why they stand so and so and why they make such and such a stroke, and the boys talking as if cricket so common in the West Indies that the babies born either with a bat or a ball, depending on if it would be a good bowler or batsman.

'That was a wonderful shot,' Charles tell Algernon grudgingly. Charles still had a feeling that the boys was only talkers, but so much controversy raging that he don't know what to say.

'If my bat didn't fly out my hand,' Algernon say, and wave his hand in the air dramatically, as if to say he would have lost the ball in the other county.

'Of course, we still have to see your bowling,' the English captain say. 'Pity about the rain – usual English weather, you know.'

'Bowling!' Algernon echo, feeling as if he is a Walcott and a Valentine roll into one. 'Oh yes, we must come back some time and finish off the match.'

'What about next Saturday?' the captain press, eager to see the boys in action again, not sure if he was dreaming about all them wild swipe and crazy strokes.

'Sure, I'll get the boys together,' Algernon say.

Algernon say that, but it wasn't possible, because none of them wanted to go back after batting, frighten that they won't be able to bowl the Englishers out.

And Charles keep reminding Algernon all the time, but Algernon keep saying how the boys scatter about, some gone Birmingham to live, and others move and gone to work somewhere else, and he can't find them anywhere.

'Never mind,' Algernon tell Charles, 'next cricket season I will get a sharp eleven together and come down your way for another match. Now, if you want me to show you how I make that stroke . . .'

Obeah in the Grove

Down by Ladbroke Grove – and I don't mean the posh part near to Holland Park, but when you start to go west: the more west you go, the more worse things get – it have a certain street, and a certain house, and in front the house have a plane tree, and one day if you pass there and you look up in the plane tree, you will see a green bottle dangling on a piece of twine, and a big bone stick up between two branch. It had a lot of other things there, and a chain of beads, but they fall down: the chain get burst and the beads scatter all about and get lost.

You want to know what them things doing up in that tree, eh? Well, I will tell you. I mean, in the West Indies, from the time you see thing like that, you know right away that somebody in for something, because thing like that mean black magic and obeah. Sometimes in the islands you get up in the morning please

God and you stretch and yawn, and when you look by your window you see some bird feather, or a piece of cloth, and right away you know that somebody trying to work a zeppy on you, somebody calling evil spirits on your head. When you look by your doorstep you see as if somebody throw a bucket of blood down there. Is time then to take steps right away to turn the evil aside, or else before you know what happening all sorts of things begin to happen, like you trip and fall down and break your hand, or else the house catch fire, or you lose your job or something. One time even it happen to a fellar that he start to swell as if he pregnant, and doctors or nobody could do anything, and everybody thought this man was going to have a baby. But that is another ballad.

Now, the latest rake when them English landlord and landlady want to sell house, is to get the tenants out, because the more empty room they have the more money they could ask for the place. And to get the tenants out, what some of them was doing was to let out rooms to spades, and when the white tenants see that they say: 'Gracious me! I can't stay in this house any longer!' and they hustle to get another room while the landlord laughing. Next thing, he give the spades notice, and by the time he ready to sell house bam! the whole house empty.

In fact, this rake was so successful that if any landlord have undesirable white tenants, the best thing was to let out couple of rooms to coloured people, and one by one the Nordics would evacuate. They used to do that, especially in them houses what have tenants from long before the war, who paying ten-twelve shillings for two-three rooms, because these days, you only have to put a put-you-up and a table and two chairs in a room and hit somebody three-four guineas a week for it.

Well this house in the Grove that I telling you about was old, I mean real old, with the paint peeling off and the roof leaking and sometimes though the sun shining the walls oozing water like a spring.

'When are we going to move,' the wife asking the man every day, 'the house will fall about our heads one day.'

'We won't get much for the place with all the flats occupied,' the man grumble.

'Jack told you what to do,' the wife say. 'Let us move out from these two rooms we have, and rent them to coloured people. Jack said when he did that, in a short time all the tenants moved and he didn't have any trouble.'

'You think Bill and Agnes will like that?' the man say. He was talking about two of the tenants: every Saturday night he and Bill used to go in the pub to play darts and drink mild and bitter, while the wife and Agnes sit down in a corner with two big glass of brown ale and gossip.

'We don't have to tell anybody anything,' the wife say. 'See how much money Jack is making these days, charging two guineas for a room that he used to get ten shillings for at one time. If even we don't get the house sold, we will be able to get good rent for the rooms.'

The very next day the wife went and put a notice up in an advertisement window by the tube station, saying that coloured people were welcome. As luck would have it, same day Agnes was passing there on the way to the Bendix with dirty clothes, and she stop by the notice board to read. I mean, it have people like that, who ain't looking for anything in particular, but they just like to stand up near them notice board and read.

'Good gracious me!' Agnes gasp when she see the

address, 'that's where I live!' and she nearly drop the bag of dirty clothes.

When she get back home she went to the wife and the wife say yes. The wife say, why shouldn't we be broad-minded, these people see so much trouble to get a place to live, we shouldn't discriminate, after all, what's wrong with coloured people. And in fact the wife outdid herself explaining to Agnes after Agnes sniff and went away, the wife stand there amazed at her own loquacity about the rights of human beings.

When the husband come home from work she tell him how Agnes take alarm and she say: 'It will work like a charm.'

She wouldn't have said that if she knew about the charm the boys was going to throw on the house in the end.

The Sunday morning, four of the boys was looking for place. They walk all the way from Paddington station reading notice board, until they land up in the Grove. The boys was Fiji, Algernon, Winky and Buttards, and all of them come from Jamaica.

Winky take a second look at the notice.

'That don't look so bad,' he say.

'It always have a catch when they say coloured people welcome,' Fiji say.

'Well we could go and see the joint,' Algernon say.

First they pass the house, giving it a once-over as they pass by.

'This house don't look good,' Algernon say.

'Is a wonder it still standing up,' Buttards say.

They turn around and start to walk again to the house.

'You go Algernon,' Winky say.

'No, you go Winky,' Algernon say.

Same time Agnes come out to go by the tube station to buy the *Pictorial* and *News of the World*, and Fiji call out 'Good morning . . .' but Agnes only sniff and pass them like a full No. 15.

'Go and ask for the landlord, man,' Buttards say, not addressing anyone in particular.

The four of them march up to the door and ring the bell. The wife come out, and as soon as she see the boys she fling the door open wide.

'Come in, come in,' she say, as if she greeting distant relatives she ain't see for a long time, and before the boys could say anything she leading them to the vacant rooms.

Well in the end the boys move in. Atmosphere tense in the house, the other tenants won't even say good morning or how do you do: in fact, in that first week two of them manage to find another place and shift out from the Grove.

'A few weeks more,' the wife tell the husband, 'and we'll be rid of them all.'

One night Buttards was having a quick one in the pub when Bill come up to him.

'You are one of the chaps living where I stay,' he say.

'Yes,' Buttards say, and wanting to make friends, he say, 'what you having?'

'Nothing,' Bill say shortly. 'But I want to tell you something. That house is going to be sold, the owner only took you coloured chaps in to get rid of us.'

And Bill leave Buttards to cogitate on those words.

Buttards cogitate, and went home to tell the boys what the position was, and then all of them start to cogitate.

'You see how it is in this country,' Buttards start to moan.

'I wasn't so keen to come here in the first place,' Winky say.

'And to think the landlady so nice to us,' Algernon say.

Only Fiji keeping quiet, and when they ask him what he have to say, he still ain't saying nothing, just sit down there working the old brains. Well when you see Fiji serious and meditating, something in the air, something brewing, and if you not Fiji friend you best hads look out, because sometimes some wild kind of plan does come to Fiji when he cogitating like that, and nothing don't stop him from doing what he plan to do.

After dinner in the evening it look like Fiji relax a little on the brain, and Winky was anxious to find out what Fiji was thinking about, so he ask him: 'What is the plan?'

'The plan is this. Take it easy, don't let them know that we know anything. In fact, treat the landlady and she husband real good, make it a real calm before the storm.'

'And what is the storm?' Buttards ask.

'The storm is this,' Fiji say, helping himself to Winky's Woods. 'We will work a little zeppy on the house. Just a little thing. Nothing much. The roof might fall in. The walls might cave in. The flooring might drop out. The whole house might tumble down one night as if the vengeance of Moko hit it. Nothing much.'

'Boy, we not back home in Jamaica now, you know,' Winky say. Winky seeing this old house falling down on him when he sleeping and he frighten.

'But what happen in Jamaica could happen here,' Fiji say.

'You mean a little obeah?' Algernon say the word at last.

'I mean a little obeah,' Fiji say after Algernon. 'Now, all of us in this together, right?'

'Right,' the others say.

'Good. Leave everything to me.'

Well in the next few days, the wife and she husband wondering what happen to the boys, they getting on so nice. When the wife going to clean out the rooms, the boys won't let her do a stroke of work. When she want to change the sheets, the boys saying is all right, they would launder the sheets themselves, she mustn't worry about a thing. Winky went so far as to buy a bunch of daffodil one evening and bring home and give to the landlady.

'Those coloured chaps must suspect something,' the wife say.

'It's just like them to try and make up to us,' the man say.

Two weeks later a big parcel come for Fiji from Jamaica. By this time everybody who white clear out of the house, and only the boys remain, with two weeks' notice hanging over their heads. In fact, the owner done have the house in the hands of a agent for sale.

'Ah, like you get something from home,' the others say to Fiji when he come home and was opening the parcel.

'I hope is pepper sauce,' Winky say.

Fiji ain't say nothing, he just open the parcel and start to take out some things one by one. When the boys see what it is that Fiji taking out, they back away.

'You know how to deal with those things, Fiji?' Buttards ask in a scared voice.

'Sure,' Fiji say. 'Ain't I say leave it to me? Now, Algernon, you went to see that place in Acton?'

'Yes,' Algernon say. 'Is all right, we could move in on the Saturday.'

'Good. Tomorrow is Friday. I not going to work. Tell the landlady I not feeling well and don't want no interruptions while I am resting. When you all come back in the evening, I will be ready. We can't afford to waste time with these things else they mightn't work.'

The next day Fiji lock himself up in the room, and stay there all day with the things he get from Jamaica. Once the landlady pass near the door and she hear as if Fiji talking to himself or singing or chanting or something, and she smell a smell as if somebody burning incense. But she ain't pay no particular attention.

When all the boys was home in the evening Fiji begin to give them instructions.

'Winky, you finish all the packing, because we have to pull out of here early in the morning – I not sure when this obeah would start to work, so we better clear out as soon as we could. Algernon, you see this here? Tonight when you get a chance, I want you to hide it over the front door – it have a ledge there. And this other thing, put it over the back door. Hide them good, so nobody won't see unless they climb up and look on the ledge. Buttards, you and I have to do the main thing.'

Fiji went to the window and open it. It had a branch of the plane tree what was near the window.

'You see that branch?' Fiji ask Buttards, 'you think you could climb up on the tree from this window?'

'I don't know about these trees in London,' Buttards start to get cagey. 'Them branch might be weak and brittle.'

'English trees is the strongest trees,' Fiji say. 'You never hear about hearts of oak?'

'What you want me to climb that tree for?'

'I want you to put some things in it. Not now, mind you. Midnight time, when nobody could see.'

Well everything went into execution that night as Fiji plan, though Buttards nearly fall down from the tree climbing in the dark, as Fiji wanted him to go to the top branch. And early the next morning the boys pull out for this other place in Acton, Fiji glancing up in the tree as they pass to make sure Buttards place all the things correctly.

Now you and me ain't going to argue about obeah. I have other things to do, and I only want to give you the episode how it happen.

Four people in all come to see the house to buy it, but all of them went away: in fact, a week later one of them was mad. Then the walls start to crack, the roof falling down bit by bit, the concrete steps under the tree in the front start to crumble. All this happening in a matter of days, mind you. Like one day the wife walking up the stairs to go to the top flat and the stairs break down and she break she foot, and the next day the husband was opening the front door and the whole door come away and nearly knock him down, and the day after that he hear that he lose his job.

The house get a kind of look about it, people afraid to even pass near it in the street. True a lot of the houses in London like that, but this one as if it threatening to collapse any minute. The landlady and she husband had was to move out and get furnished rooms, and the agent say he washing his hands of the matter, that it look as if the house have a jinx, that nobody want to buy it.

Well, is winter now and all the leaves fall off the trees, so if by chance you ever liming in the Grove and you want to see for yourself, just go in that certain street. You can't miss the house at all, and you will see that bottle dangling from the top branch where Buttards nearly fall down when he was putting it there in the dark.

Only thing, mind and don't pass too near, 'cause that house have the vengeance of Moko on it and it might tumble down any time.

My Girl and the City

All these words that I hope to write, I have written them already many times in my mind. I have had many beginnings, each as good or as bad as the other. Hurtling in the underground from station to station, mind the doors, missed it!, there is no substitute for wool: waiting for a bus in Piccadilly Circus: walking across Waterloo bridge: watching the bed of the Thames when the tide is out – choose one, choose a time, a place, any time or any place, and take off, as if this were interrupted conversation, as if you and I were earnest friends and there is no need for preliminary remark.

One day of any day it is like this. I wait for my girl on Waterloo bridge, and when she comes there is a mighty wind blowing across the river, and we lean against it and laugh, her skirt skylarking, her hair whipping across her face.

I wooed my girl, mostly on her way home from work, and I talked a great deal. Often, it was as if I had never spoken, I heard my words echo in deep caverns of thought, as if they hung about like cigarette smoke in a still room, missionless; or else they were lost for ever in the sounds of the city.

We used to wait for a 196 under the railway bridge across the Waterloo road. There were always long queues and it looked like we would never get a bus. Fidgeting in that line of impatient humanity I got in precious words edgeways, and a train would rumble and drown my words in thundering steel. Still, it was important to talk. In the crowded bus, as if I wooed three or four instead of one, I shot words over my shoulder, across seats; once past a bespectacled man reading the *Evening News* who lowered his paper and eyed me that I was mad. My words bumped against people's faces, on the glass window of the bus; they found passage between 'fares please' and once I got to writing things on a piece of paper and pushing my hand over two seats.

The journey ended and there was urgent need to communicate before we parted.

All these things I say, I said, waving my hand in

the air as if to catch the words floating about me and give them mission. I say them because I want you to know, I don't ever want to regret afterwards that I didn't say enough, I would rather say too much.

Take that Saturday evening, I am waiting for her in Victoria station. When she comes we take the Northern Line to Belsize Park (I know a way to the heath from there, I said). When we get out of the lift and step outside there is a sudden downpour and everyone scampers back into the station. We wait a while, then go out in it. We get lost. I say, Let us ask that fellow the way. But she says No, fancy asking someone the way to the heath on this rainy night, just find out how to get back to the tube station.

We go back, I get my bearings afresh, and we set off. She is hungry. Wait here, I say under a tree at the side of the road, and I go to a pub for some sandwiches. Water slips off me and makes puddles on the counter as I place my order. The man is taking a long time and I go to the door and wave to her across the street signifying I shan't be too long.

When I go out she has crossed the road and is sheltering in a doorway pouting. You leave me standing in the rain and stay such a long time, she says. I had to wait for the sandwiches, I say, what do you think, I was having a quick one? Yes, she says.

We walk on through the rain and we get to the heath and the rain is falling slantways and carefree and miserable. For a minute we move around in an indecisive way as if we're looking for some particular spot. Then we see a tree which might offer some shelter and we go there and sit on a bench wet and bedraggled.

I am sorry for all this rain, I say, as if I were responsible. I take off her raincoat and make her put on my quilted jacket. She takes off her soaking shoes and tucks her feet under her skirt on the bench. She tries to dry her hair with a handkerchief. I offer her the sandwiches and light a cigarette for myself. Go on, have one, she says. I take a half and munch it, and smoke.

It is cold there. The wind is raging in the leaves of the trees, and the rain is pelting. But abruptly it ceases, the clouds break up in the sky, and the moon shines. When the moon shines, it shines on her face, and I look at her, the beauty of her washed by rain, and I think many things.

Suddenly we are kissing and I wish I could die there and then and there's an end to everything, to all the Jesus-Christ thoughts that make up every moment of my existence.

Writing all this now – and some weeks have gone by since I started – it is lifeless and insipid and useless. Only at the time, there was something, a thought that propelled me. Always, in looking back, there was something, and at the time I am aware of it, and the creation goes on and on in my mind while I look at all the faces around me in the tube, the restless rustle of newspapers, the hiss of air as the doors close, the enaction of life in a variety of form.

Once I told her and she said, as she was a stenographer, that she would come with me and we would ride the Inner Circle and I would just voice my thoughts and she would write them down, and that way we could make something of it. Once the train was crowded and she sat opposite to me and after a while I looked at her and she smiled and turned away. What is all this, what is the meaning of all these things that happen to people, the movement from one place to another, lighting a cigarette, slipping a coin into a slot and pulling a drawer for chocolate, buying a return ticket, waiting for a bus, working the crossword puzzle in the *Evening Standard*?

Sometimes you are in the underground and you have no idea what the weather is like, and the train shoots out of a tunnel and sunlight floods you, falls across your newspaper, makes the passengers squint and look up.

There is a face you have for sitting at home and talking, there is a face you have for working in the office, there is a face, a bearing, a demeanour for each time and place. There is above all a face for travelling, and when you have seen one you have seen all. In a rush hour, when we are breathing down each other's necks, we look at each other and glance quickly away. There is not a great deal to look at in the narrow confines of a carriage except people, and the faces of people, but no one deserves a glass of Hall's wine more than you do. We jostle in the subway from train to lift, we wait, shifting our feet. When we are all herded inside we hear the footsteps of a straggler for whom the operator waits, and we try to figure out what sort of a footstep it is, if he feels the lift will wait for him; we are glad if he is left waiting while we shoot upward. Out of the lift, down the street, up the road: in ten seconds flat it is over, and we have to begin again.

One morning I am coming into the city by the 287 night bus from Streatham. It is after one o'clock; I have been stranded again after seeing my girl home. When we get to Westminster bridge the sky is marvellously clear with a few stray patches of beautiful cloud among which stars sparkle. The moon stands over Waterloo bridge, above the Houses of Parliament sharply outlined, and it throws gold on the waters of the Thames. The Embankment is quiet, only a few people loiter around the public convenience near to the Charing Cross underground which is open all night. A man sleeps on a bench. His head is resting under headlines: Suez Deadlock.

Going back to that same spot about five o'clock in the evening, there was absolutely nothing to recall the atmosphere of the early morning hours. Life had taken over completely, and there was nothing but people. People waiting for buses, people hustling for trains.

I go to Waterloo bridge and they come pouring out of the offices and they bob up and down as they walk across the bridge. From the station green trains come and go relentlessly. Motion mesmerises me into immobility. There are lines of motion across the river, on the river.

Sometimes we sat on a bench near the river, and if the tide was out you could see the muddy bed of the river and the swans grubbing. Such spots, when found, are pleasant to loiter in. Sitting in one of those places – choose one, and choose a time – where it is possible to escape for a brief spell from Christ and the cup of tea, I have known a great frustration and weariness. All these things, said, have been said before, the river seen, the skirt pressed against the swelling thigh noted, the lunch hour eating apples in the sphinx's lap under Cleopatra's Needle observed and duly registered: even to talk of the frustration is a repetition. What am I to do, am I to take each circumstance, each thing seen, noted, and mill them in my mind and spit out something entirely different from the reality?

My girl is very real. She hated the city, I don't know why. It's like that sometimes, a person doesn't have to have a reason. A lot of people don't like London that way, you ask them why and they shrug, and a shrug is sometimes a powerful reply to a question.

She shrugged when I asked her why, and when she asked me why I loved London I too shrugged. But after a minute I thought I would try to explain, because too a shrug is an easy way out of a lot of things.

Falteringly I told her how one night it was late and I found a fish and chips shop open in the East End and I bought and ate in the dark street walking; and of the cup of tea in an all-night café in Kensington one grim winter morning; and of the first time I ever queued in this country in '50 to see the Swan Lake ballet, and the friend who was with me gave a busker two and six because he was playing Sentimental Journey on a mouth-organ.

But why do you love London, she said.

You can't talk about a thing like that, not really. Maybe I could have told her because one evening in the summer I was waiting for her, only it wasn't like summer at all. Rain had been falling all day, and a haze hung about the bridges across the river, and the water was muddy and brown, and there was a kind of wistfulness and sadness about the evening. The way St Paul's was half-hidden in the rain, the motionless trees along the Embankment. But you say a thing like that and people don't understand at all. How sometimes a surge of greatness could sweep over you when you see something.

But even if I had said all that and much more, it would not have been what I meant. You could be lonely as hell in the city, then one day you look around you and you realise everybody else is lonely too, withdrawn, locked, rushing home out of the chaos: blank faces, unseeing eyes, millions and millions of them, up the Strand, down the Strand, jostling in Charing Cross for the 5.20: in Victoria station, a pretty continental girl wearing a light, becoming shade of lipstick stands away from the board on which the departures of trains appear and cocks her head sideways, hands thrust into pockets of a fawn raincoat.

I catch the eyes of this girl with my own: we each register sight, appreciation: we look away, our eyes pick up casual station activities: she turns to an automatic refreshment machine, hesitant, not sure if she would be able to operate it.

Things happen, and are finished with for ever: I did not talk to her, I did not look her way again, or even think of her.

I look on the wall of the station at the clock, it is after half-past eight, and my girl was to have met me at six o'clock. I feel in my pockets for pennies to telephone. I only have two. I ask change of a stander with the usual embarrassment: when I telephone, the line is engaged. I alternate between standing in the spot we have arranged to meet and telephoning, but each time the line is engaged. I call the exchange: they ascertain that something is wrong with the line.

At ten minutes to nine I am eating a corned-beef sandwich when she comes. Suddenly now nothing matters except that she is here. She never expected that I would still be waiting, but she came on the off-chance. I never expected that she would come, but I waited on the off-chance.

Now I have a different word for this thing that happened – an off-chance, but that does not explain why it happens, and what it is that really happens. We go to St James's Park, we sit under a tree, we kiss, the moon can be seen between leaves.

Wooing my way towards, sometimes in our casual conversation we came near to great, fundamental truths, and it was a little frightening. It wasn't like wooing at all, it was more discussion of when will it end, and must it ever end, and how did it begin, and how will it go on from here? We scattered words on the green summer grass, under trees, on dry leaves in a wood of quivering aspens, and sometimes it was as if I was struck speechless with too much to say, and held my tongue between thoughts frightened of utterance.

Once again I am on a green train returning to the heart from the suburbs, and I look out of the window into windows of private lives flashed on my brain. Bread being sliced, a man taking off a jacket, an old woman knitting. And all these things I see – the curve of a woman's arm, undressing, the blankets being tucked, and once a solitary figure staring at trains as I stared at windows. All the way into London Bridge – is falling down, is falling down, the wheels say: one must have a thought – where buildings and the shadows of them encroach on the railway tracks. Now the train crawls across the bridges, dark steel in the darkness: the thoughtful gloom of Waterloo: Charing Cross bridge, Thames reflecting lights, and the silhouettes of city buildings against the sky of the night.

When I was in New York, many times I went into that city late at night after a sally to the outskirts, it lighted up with a million lights, but never a feeling as on entering London. Each return to the city is loaded with thought, so that by the time I take the Inner Circle I am as light as air.

At last I think I know what it is all about. I move around in a world of words. Everything that happens is words. But pure expression is nothing. One must build on the things that happen: it is insufficient to say I sat in the underground and the train hurtled through the darkness and someone isn't using Amplex. So what? So now I weave, I say there was an old man on whose face wrinkles rivered, whose hands were shapeful with arthritis but when he spoke, oddly enough, his voice was young and gay.

But there was no old man, there was nothing, and there is never ever anything.

My girl, she is beautiful to look at. I have seen her in sunlight and in moonlight, and her face carves an exquisite shape in darkness.

These things we talk, I burst out, why mustn't I say them? If I love you, why shouldn't I tell you so?

I love London, she said.

Ryūnosuke Akutagawa · *Hell Screen* · 9780241573693

Elizabeth von Arnim · *The Enchanted April* · 9780241619742

Jane Austen · *Lady Susan* · 9780241582527

Karen Blixen · *Babette's Feast* · 9780241597286

Jorge Luis Borges · *The Library of Babel* · 9780241630860

Italo Calvino · *Cosmicomics* · 9780241573709

Albert Camus · *The Fall* · 9780241630778

Truman Capote · *Breakfast at Tiffany's* · 9780241597262

Anton Chekhov · *About Love* · 9780241619766

Kate Chopin · *The Awakening* · 9780241630785

Joseph Conrad · *The Lagoon* · 9780241619773

Fyodor Dostoyevsky · *White Nights* · 9780241619780

Arthur Conan Doyle · *The Adventure of the
    Blue Carbuncle* · 9780241597002

F. Scott Fitzgerald · *Babylon Revisited* · 9780241630839

Kahlil Gibran · *The Prophet* · 9780241573716

Lafcadio Hearn · *Of Ghosts and Goblins* · 9780241573723

O. Henry · *The Gift of the Magi* · 9780241597019

E. T. A. Hoffmann · *The Nutcracker* · 9780241597064

Shirley Jackson · *The Lottery* · 9780241590539

Franz Kafka · *Metamorphosis* · 9780241573730

Anna Kavan · *Ice* · 9780241597330

Yasunari Kawabata · *Snow Country* · 9780241597361

Nella Larsen · *Passing* · 9780241573747

Clarice Lispector · *The Imitation of the Rose* · 9780241630846

Katherine Mansfield · *Bliss* · 9780241619797

For rights reasons, not all titles available in the USA and Canada.